STRENGTH OF HER HEART

KIT KENNETH

MCKINNEY AVENUE PUBLISHING

Print ISBN: 978-0-578-45739-0

Ebook ISBN: 978-0-578-45745-1

This is a work of fiction. Names, characters, places, and incidents either are the products of the author's imagination or are used fictitiously. Any resemblance to actual persons, living or dead, businesses, companies, events, or locales is entirely coincidental.

Editing by Paige Duke & Erin Servais / Standout Books

Design and layout by Standout Books

Published by McKinney Avenue Publishing

"I'm having a girl!" Barb exclaimed loudly as she announced her news to her two sisters over dinner one night at her house in Dallas. Barb was beaming with excitement. She had been blessed with baby number two, but this time she was having a girl.

"Congratulations, sister! I couldn't be happier for you," Dee said as she hugged Barb tightly.

"Yes, congratulations. We can't wait to meet her," Kate echoed.

Dee and Kate never had any desire to have children. It wasn't that thing that most women felt they had to have in their life . . . the need to reproduce. For Barb it was different. She waited her whole life to become a parent, and her two sisters had never seen her happier. She was fulfilling the life she had dreamed up, and now this baby girl would complete the perfect family she wished for all those years ago. The sisters were already blessed with their nephew, who was just two years old. Their only hope was that he'd come to follow his father's footsteps one day.

Barb continued to ramble on about the pregnancy and all the excitement behind bringing a little girl into the world as she walked out of the room to tend to her son, Trenton, who was playing in the other room nearby.

Dee turned to Kate, "To Barb's baby . . . we have another girl to welcome into the family. Let's just hope she doesn't inherit what we've had to live with," she said as she cheersed Kate's wine glass.

SANTA CLAUSE IS COMING
TO TOWN

Clink, clink, clink. The noise of the tinkling champagne glasses filled the room. But the sound was interrupted by a loud crash of glass shattering on the kitchen floor.

"Damn it, Barb, you're so damn clumsy!" DeeAnna yelled, racing to clean up the shattered glass. Dee knelt down and picked up the debris piece by piece, a Marlboro light hanging out of her mouth.

Barb, completely unfazed by the fact that she had just shattered four crystal champagne flutes, roared with laughter as she reached for a different glass in her newly painted white cabinets. Barb stumbled over to the giant bowl of eggnog she'd made earlier that day and filled her glass to the top.

Kate sat at the kitchen bar and just shook her head at her two older sisters while she sipped her pinot grigio. She'd been eyeing the grand display of desserts Barb had set out on the back table when the crash interrupted her.

Though Kate didn't agree with much in Barb's life, she did enjoy Barb's desserts. She watched Dee scrape up the broken champagne flutes, toss them in the trash, and wipe whatever was left of the Moët champagne from the floor. Luckily, Barb had already consumed most of the leftover champagne as she'd carried it from the dining room to the kitchen.

Barb had been cooking for three days—and she made sure her two sisters knew it. Now it was her time to sit back and relax while she made her older sister, Dee, do all the dishes. Dee proudly embraced her job as dishwasher. She could barely cook, so washing dishes was her contribution to helping out at family gatherings.

"You know, I'd be able to sit and relax a lot sooner if Barb hadn't used every fucking dish in this kitchen to cook with. She's made a damn mess!" Dee chuckled to her youngest sister, Kate. Dee's thick, curly brown hair was pulled back into a hair tie, and her glasses barely rested on the tip of her nose.

Kate giggled at Dee but continued to stare off into space. She sat poised in her chair, her back perfectly straight thanks to years of ballet. Kate never slouched or appeared lazy with the way she carried herself. Her mental posture was not so orderly. She found herself drifting away into her thoughts, barely paying attention to Dee muttering over the dishes. She had a lot on her mind these days. Kate chalked it up to being in her early thirties, a natural time to be contemplating her life's path.

"And what's with the paper-thin fine china? What are we, the royal family? This shit won't even go in the dishwasher! I'm going to be here all damn night." Dee continued muttering over the sink, regardless if anyone could hear her or not. The truth was Dee loved Barb's taste for the finer things in life, but she also loved teasing her little sisters and making them laugh.

"Now, now, Barb's china is gorgeous. She wanted to have a nice Christmas dinner for all of us, and that's exactly what we had. Be thankful you have a sister who is such an incredible cook and has hosted such a lovely evening," Lillian said as she emerged in the kitchen, gin and tonic in hand, to join her three daughters.

Kate rolled her eyes just as she always did when Lillian praised Barb. To Kate, Barb was the lucky one; she always had it so easy. Barb was married to a dashing, up-and-coming businessman and lived in a beautiful home with two beautiful children. She had the dream.

The Harold women remained in the kitchen long after the Christmas Eve festivities died down and Barb's two kids were put to bed. Dee carried on washing dishes and cursing every piece of silver, cutting board, china, and high-end knife that Barb made her hand wash.

"I don't understand why you wear your hair like that. It really doesn't show the shape of your face," Barb said to Kate.

Kate pretended she didn't hear Barb's observation as Barb carried on.

"Well, life is pretty amazing these days. I've got a great house, my own business, and great kids," Barb said as she looked around at her newly remodeled kitchen. "What's up next for you, Kate?"

"Work is a beating, and my only real escape these days is my ballet classes." Kate shrugged as she looked away from her sister.

"Well, Kate, one day maybe you can be as happy as me."

Kate sat unamused by Barb's comments. The truth was Kate did not know if she was happy or not. She didn't know what she wanted. Dee saw the look of frustration on her youngest sister's face.

"Barb, let off little Kate. A white picket fence and perfect family is not everyone's fairy tale. You have your version of happiness and Kate has hers."

Barb was always striving for perfection between her job and family, while Kate just longed for a comfortable life on her own away from the family drama. Both had different viewpoints on what happiness and success looked like. This was probably why they were always at odds with one another. Dee always came to the rescue between them, but she found herself caught up in the drama of it all instead of helping. Lillian gave up trying to keep the peace between her three daughters long ago, and now she just let them duke it out whenever they decided to test each other.

The men of the family were outside on Barb's husband Mickey's new patio having cigars and admiring the new stone Mickey had just put in. Mickey had spent the entire summer and fall completely redoing the deck in his backyard. What started as his pet project had to be handed over to a contractor. Mickey was always torn between projects at the house and building his business. He never liked asking for help, but had finally given in after Barb stayed on him about the backyard being a mess.

The men of the family always separated quickly after dinner, most likely to get away from the Harold women drama. When enough wine was consumed, you never knew what kind of hell would break loose, so the men knew best to keep their distance. They rarely had interest in seeing what the women would argue about next.

Through the clinking of glass and the bickering of four drunk women, somehow Ophelia, Barb's youngest child and only daughter, slept soundly on the couch in the living room by the fire. She was completely unaware of everything happening in the next room.

Dee, Barb, and Kate had tucked Ophelia in on the couch earlier that night, burying her like a peaceful little mummy underneath big flannel blankets after the family finished opening presents. Ophelia's golden hair was wrapped around her little face, and the blankets were pulled up underneath her chin to ward off the cold night— rare for Texas even at this time of year. Ophelia slept soundly with a smile on her perfectly round face.

Barb and the aunts promised her this would be the year she would get to meet Santa Claus. They had told her that if she was a good girl and went to sleep early that night, they would wake her when he arrived.

Ophelia had been running back and forth throughout the house all day trying to pass the time.

"Santa only comes at night, right Daddy?"

"Yes, princess. You're going to have to wait a little longer," Mickey said. "Now that you're eight, it's time meet the man in red."

"I know, Daddy! I'm *so* excited. I hope I can fall asleep. I might be *too* excited," she said, her eyes bright and full of hope.

She knew Santa always promised goodwill and fortune for all those who were good to each other that year.

Mickey leaned in and gave Ophelia's arm a gentle squeeze. "Well, you know what they say about Santa's list. Think you've been a good girl this year?"

"Daddy, you know I have! I only fought with Trenton a few times. I've been working on my manners."

Mickey laughed. "I know you have. You'll be on the nice list. No doubt."

Ophelia wasn't worried. She loved her family and her classmates and always made sure to treat everyone with kindness. She couldn't wait to tell Santa all about it and tell him all about her family. She also couldn't wait to see what he'd brought her this year. Every time Santa Claus would drop the gift during the night while she slept. She knew he was a very busy man. He had a lot of children to visit that night, after all. But tonight, Barb and the aunts had promised he was going to hand-deliver the gift himself.

Ophelia would finally meet the man who made Christmas dreams come true. Santa had always been Ophelia's hero. She couldn't believe that a man was capable of making so many miracles happen for so many people! She admired his kindness and compassion for everyone. And all he wanted to do was give to others. The hope of Christmas was all wrapped up in what Santa brought to the world that night. Ophelia believed in magic and knew Santa was there to make all her dreams come true.

The events of the day and night wore her out. The annual Christmas Eve event at her house was Ophelia's favorite time of year. She always looked forward to it, especially in the weeks leading up to it when the whole world seemed to be prepping for the holiday season. The trees, the Christmas carols, the lights, the joy of wishing a stranger on the street a Merry Christmas all filled Ophelia with so much love that she wanted to share it with everyone.

That morning, Ophelia's feet hit the ground only a moment after she opened her eyes. She grinned at the smells of Christmas dinner being prepared in the kitchen. Waking to the smell of her mother's cooking on Christmas Eve morning was one of her favorite things. She bounced happily into the kitchen and greeted her mother.

"Morning," Barb huffed, blowing a stray hair from her face. She was on day three of her annual preparation of the great Christmas Eve feast for the family. She had spent the morning making all the appetizers: her famous homemade cheeseball and meatballs. Her turkey was also already roasting in the oven. Though she was only expecting nine for the party, she always cooked for twenty.

Ophelia barreled into her for a tight hug, but Barb's hands were too sticky to squeeze back. Only after her daughter left the kitchen did she clean her hands and dry them on her apron—her favorite apron with Santa Claus that always put her in the Christmas spirit—carefully protecting the perfect Christmas sweater she'd donned that morning. She'd paired it with leggings that clung to her long, skinny legs. Her elongated necklace adorned in snowmen, peppermint canes, and bells jingled happily against her chest, where she'd tucked it away from dangling into the food.

Barb was wrapping up the appetizers to put away for later when Ophelia came bouncing back into the kitchen. "Can I help, Mom? Pleeeeease!" said Ophelia with a huge grin on her face. She was missing both her front teeth, which made Barb giggle at her huge grin.

"You sure can, my little princess!" "Princess" was the nickname Lillian and the aunts had given Ophelia the day she was born. She was the youngest in the family, after all.

"I'm about to make my famous chocolate and vanilla cake. Why don't you run outside and pick out your favorite leaves?" said Barb as she cupped her hand underneath her chin.

She knew it was Ophelia's favorite part of helping, determined to pick the best leaves from the front yard. Barb used the leaves to shape chocolate leaves to adorn the top of the cake like a circular crown. Ophelia called it her Princess Cake. Ophelia was always amazed at how Barb made the leaves look so realistic. Barb would take the leaves and dip them into melted chocolate only to harden later. She'd then peel off the real leaf once the chocolate took form.

She never actually cared much for the cake itself; she just enjoyed picking and eating the chocolate leaves that sat on top of the cake. Barb smiled, thinking of how her daughter always managed to eat the entire chocolate crown.

Ophelia ran out the back door as Barb yelled after her

to put on a jacket. She liked this project much better than the project her mother had given her the previous day, when she was stuck polishing the massive silver collection for several hours. Her mother always served Christmas Eve dinner using the best china and silver, and she wanted Ophelia to have everything in pristine condition before the rest of the family arrived. O's hands were bright red by the time she'd finished rubbing each piece of silver. And if she tried to cut corners, her mother would make Ophelia go back and polish any piece that was not to her satisfaction. Ophelia could tell her mother took pride in cooking and preparing Christmas dinner every year. As young as she was, she understood this was why her mother hosted the family at their house.

Barb was a natural host for the family events. And like Ophelia, Barb loved Christmas more than any other time of year. It was a time to bring her family together and to get her kids, Trenton and Ophelia, into the Christmas spirit. The house she and Mickey had spent so much time and money to remodel was always perfectly decorated for the season. The courtyard leading up to their front door was covered in a jungle of poinsettias. It was her favorite place to snap pictures of Trenton and Ophelia in the Christmas outfits she bought for them. She'd taken care to wrap the grand columns in the entryway in nutcracker ribbon. Garland lined the top of the five large windows at the front of the house that gave a beautiful view of the grand piano Barb loved to play. She had placed a candle on each windowsill and lit them every night so the house glowed from the street.

The grand Christmas tree sat in the same spot in the

living room where she put it every year and was covered in white powder. Ophelia had always loved that since they rarely had a white Christmas in Texas. And on the rare occasion they did, it never stuck to the ground, so the white faux snow tree made both Barb and Ophelia feel closer to that imaginary winter wonderland.

Ophelia always dreamed of a white Christmas year over year. Barb knew it was the piece of Christmas she always missed the most. Trenton's train was wrapped around the tree, as usual, breaking down due to age or just from the family cat knocking the train off course while trying to whack the ball-shaped ornaments off the tree. She smiled, thinking how Trenton and Ophelia always placed the smaller gifts on the train cars and loved to watch them make their circle over and over again around the tree.

When the timer dinged, Barb donned her Christmas oven mitts, warmed by the site of the teddy bears smiling up at her. The Christmas teddy bears. Barb always covered the house in teddy bears at Christmastime. She wasn't shy about admitting them as her signature decoration. They were just so cheery and cuddly, greeting you when you walked into the entryway of the house, smiling down at you from shelves, standing in a line like a choir underneath the grand piano, and staring out at the festivities from their perches all over the tree. Any time she saw a Christmas teddy bear, Barb bought it and put it somewhere in the house during the holidays. Most of the teddy bears had some sort of significant value or meaning from some past year, but only Barb knew the stories.

For some reason, that made Barb think of her mother, and her smile slipped. Lillian arrived the previous day, driving in from Abilene with her two lapdogs. Those animals didn't like anyone but her mother, and they rarely ever left her side. They'd snap at you if you came within five feet of her. Barb couldn't believe the number of bags she'd dragged in with her. You'd think the woman was staying for weeks, not the mere two nights they'd agreed on. If Barb knew her mother, only one of the bags contained clothes. In the others, she'd be carrying cameras, binoculars, books, magazines, dog toys, dog food, and whatever else she felt like hauling over from her home.

Barb tried to be grateful, though. She knew her mother came to stay to be near her only two grandchildren. And this year would be hard, the first year without her husband. Carl had passed away earlier that year. Lillian was adjusting to her life on her own and put most of her energy and attention toward plotting out her travels across the great west while enjoying time with her grandchildren.

Her mother was coping as best she could. She'd always had her little luxuries. Barb snorted a laugh, remembering how Lillian taught Trenton how to properly make his grandmother her gin and tonic the night before. "Well, he's eleven now, Barb," Lillian said as if that explained it all. "It's time my grandson learns how to prepare his grand-mother's signature drink."

Between bartending sessions with Trenton, she'd spend most of the afternoon reading her books while Barb banged around in the kitchen. Her mother never felt the need to assist her. But then Barb never really needed help. She prided herself on keeping things very organized and sticking to her routine. By way of explanation, her mother had said, "I'll just relax, dear. We both know I'll only be in your way if I try to help."

Dee arrived shortly after that. She was always the first of Barb's sisters to arrive. She and her husband, Chuck, made a grand and noticeable entrance that made Ophelia jump with excitement. Chuck swung open the front door only to have all four of their dogs come pouring into the house.

"Get the back door, O! They're coming in!" yelled Chuck. O went running to the back sliding glass door to ensure the gang of dogs emptied securely into the back-yard to join the two Labradors that Mickey and Barb had bought for Trenton and Ophelia. Six regular dogs plus Lillian's two lapdogs always turned Mickey and Barb's backyard into an animal playpen. Barb and Mickey never invited the dogs, but Dee and Chuck never spent a holiday without their four-legged children.

Barb wasn't surprised when Chuck immediately joined Mickey out on the back patio. She never quite understood their connection; they were such complete opposites. They must have found a common bond being married to Harold sisters, Barb wondered more than once. As usual, Dee was five minutes behind Chuck coming into the house and was carrying a Tom Thumb bag full of all the ingredients Barb asked her to pick up that she had forgotten. And, of course, she had her Marlboro Lights and the dogs' leashes in tow. In the other hand, Dee lugged her box of Franzia wine Barb knew her sister would singlehandedly devour by the end of the night. Never mind the high-end wines she and Mickey stocked, Dee preferred her wine straight from the box.

Always last to arrive was Kate. Fashionable Kate was always fashionably late. Kate never had a great concept of time and always strolled in when she wanted to. She was never in a hurry to be anywhere. This time, though, Barb could tell something had happened. Her sister's eyes were bloodshot, her cheeks a little pink. She'd been crying. Behind her was her boyfriend, Jet. He was visibly frustrated and was carrying all the presents while Kate barely said anything. The two must have argued the entire way over, and Barb was willing to bet they'd spend the rest of the night bickering at one another. From something Kate had said on the phone, Barb wouldn't be surprised if this was their last Christmas together. Kate hadn't seemed too torn up about it either. Barb knew when her sister was putting on a brave face to get her through the night. It was too bad. Jet was a friend of hers and Mickey's. They'd been the ones to set him up with Kate, and Barb thought they were perfect for one another. According to Barb, Kate always had a way of sabotaging a good thing that came her way.

Ophelia lit up at the sight of Aunt Kate. She came running up to both of them. Jet immediately picked up O and swung her in the air. Ophelia always liked Jet, but even she could see he never made Kate smile. Every time she saw Kate with him, she looked sad.

Jet was a powerful businessman looking for a wife. He was drawn to Kate's natural beauty and saw her as the trophy wife he always wanted. Kate wouldn't have it, though. The idea of just being someone's wife made Kate miserable inside. She had much more to offer.

"Jet, promise you'll dance with me later?" Ophelia asked in a high-pitched voice.

"You bet, kiddo! I couldn't not dance with the most beautiful girl in the world!" he said, pushing Ophelia up high into the air.

He put her down next to Kate and walked outside to join Mickey and Chuck. Ophelia's attention then turned toward Kate. She knew Kate was hurting but didn't quite understand why. Kate gave O a huge squeeze as she took her in her arms and held her for what seemed like two minutes. Ophelia finally stepped back and looked into Kate's sad eyes.

"What's wrong, Auntie Kate?" O asked.

"Nothing that a glass of wine won't fix, my love!" replied Kate as she gave her a little Eskimo kiss.

Ophelia giggled and assured Kate it was going to be a great Christmas. Kate and Ophelia had always shared a special bond. They knew how to cheer each other up. Kate didn't have children of her own, nor did she ever think she'd want any, but Ophelia was her special little someone. They'd bonded the instant Ophelia was born. Ophelia's bright, shiny smile always made Kate forget about the bad times, including the fight she'd had with Jet on the way over.

The whole family settled in, and soon it was time to head down the street for the Christmas Eve service at Barb and Mickey's church. As usual, Dee and Chuck would not be attending. O never understood why, but they always told her someone had to stay behind and look after the four-legged family members. Everyone else loaded up in Mickey's Suburban and headed down the street.

Barb wanted pictures of O and Trenton at the front of the church, where all the poinsettias sat and adorned the church alter. The twenty-five pictures Barb had taken earlier in the day in the courtyard where not enough.

"More Poinsettia pictures?!" Trenton growled as he rolled his eyes.

"Yeah, Mom, more?!" Ophelia echoed Trenton and rolled her eyes, as well. She always copied what Trenton did. He was the coolest and funniest person Ophelia knew.

Barb had dressed O in a white blouse with shoulder pads and a big poufy black velvet skirt. O hated her outfit. A natural tomboy, Ophelia preferred her leggings and oversized Christmas sweater. The more she complained, though, the louder Barb's voice would grow, so Ophelia would sink down and stay quiet to avoid further embarrassment.

Kate agreed that Ophelia looked ridiculous, especially having an eight year old wear shoulder pads. "Just let her get her Christmas photo of you and Trenton, and then you can go back to putting on whatever you want." Kate winked. Ophelia grinned back and gave a huge smile for the picture.

After the service, everyone headed back to the house for dinner. By this time Aunt Dee was already halfway through her boxed wine and one-third of the way through her box of Marlboro lights. Barb put on music so loud it blared throughout the house and the family spent the first ten minutes of dinner shouting over each other until Lillian finally yelled at Barb, "Turn the damn music down!"

Barb and Mickey sat at the head of each side of the

grand dining room table that Barb had carefully decorated with candles, ribbon, and name plates. Lillian sat on one side with Trenton and O between her. Kate, Jet, Dee, and Chuck had been placed on the other side. Several bottles of wine sat between family members, who indulged in swapping reasons why Texas was the greatest state to live in and other usual Republican politics.

Halfway through dinner, everyone realized something was burning.

"I knew it!" yelled Lillian. "You girls burned the damn bread again!"

Dee, Barb, and Kate all looked at one other, trying to remember who was in charge of making sure the bread made it out of the oven. It was a Harold female tradition to burn the bread. Whoever put it in the oven usually forgot about it.

Dee ran to recover the charred bread from the kitchen. "Well, no one is getting any bread again this year," she exclaimed as she came back into the dining room.

"You women are a bunch of dumbasses sometimes," remarked Chuck.

As usual, dinner was followed by the gift exchanges. O and Trenton were covered in gifts from the family. Dee and Kate never had children, so O and Trenton were their surrogate kids. O and Trenton never doubted they'd get everything they asked for on the Christmas lists Barb had them write out each year. Mickey and Barb worked hard to ensure their children's Christmas wishes were always granted. But more than anything, Ophelia and Trenton delighted in seeing what Santa brought them on Christmas morning. That was always the big surprise!

This year was no different—they couldn't wait to see what Santa had in store for them tomorrow.

Earlier in the evening, Ophelia received a phone call from Santa himself. "Ho ho ho! Merry Christmas, Ophelia! I'm headed to Texas!" Bells rang in the background. Her heart skipped a beat as she imagined the reindeer shaking their furry heads. Ophelia could not contain her excitement. She told Santa to be safe and that she couldn't wait to meet him. She hung up the phone and immediately ran to tell Trenton.

In preparation for Santa's grand arrival, Trenton helped Ophelia set out the cookies and milk on the fireplace mantel. O picked out the best pieces from the tray of decorated sugar cookies, remembering how Barb let her help make them the day before. Her mother prepared the cookie dough from scratch, and then she handed it over to Ophelia, along with all the Christmas cookie cutter shapes, to create the cookies. O had laid them all out on the counter: the reindeer, the Santa, the Nutcracker, the Sugar Plum Fairy, a bell, a star, and a stocking. After her mother helped her make the shapes, they'd put them in the oven together. Once the cookies were baked, O was allowed to use the icing tools to decorate them.

Inspecting the tray by the firelight, Ophelia picked out the reindeer, stocking, and Santa decorated in red and green icing to give to the big man in red. She made sure Trenton approved of her cookie choices, and he assured her Santa would love them.

Barb and the aunts tucked Ophelia in on the couch before returning to the kitchen. She fell asleep with a big smile on her face. Her dreams of meeting Santa Claus would come true tonight. She knew he was a busy man and wouldn't have too much time to spend with her. There were other kids in the world waiting for him to deliver their gifts too. But tonight he'd set aside an extra few minutes just to meet her.

Hours into their wine-drinking, arguing, and dishwashing, Barb, Dee, and Kate, realizing it was getting late, stumbled into the living room to wake Ophelia. They had begrudgingly agreed to take a break from their duties to keep their promise to Ophelia.

"Is it time to tell her?" Dee asked Barb. Dee was polishing off the last of her box wine.

"Yes, she's old enough now to know," Barb said.

"Okay, girls . . . take it easy on her. You're not sure how she'll react," Lillian warned her daughters.

"Mom! She's my daughter! She'll be fine. Ophelia is a tough little cookie," Barb snapped back at Lillian.

It was a few minutes after midnight, and O sat up, dazed from her dream but beaming in excitement, looking at her two aunts and mother sitting by her side.

"Is he here?!" yelled Ophelia. Her eyes searched the living room, wondering where Santa could be. She looked at the fireplace, which still had a fire roaring, and then looked into her mother and aunts' puffy eyes.

"Well, honey, we woke you up to tell you that Santa is not real," Barb explained slowly.

"What?!" Ophelia's voice grew loud.

"It's all made up. There is no Santa Claus," Dee echoed.

Ophelia stared blankly at her mother and looked at Dee and Kate one by one. They just nodded in agreement as they all sat around her. Ophelia's chest tightened, and tears welled up in her eyes. She was crying so hard she couldn't speak. Every dream and vision she'd had of that big, jolly man in a red suit who climbed down her chimney to spread Christmas cheer was a huge lie. All the faith she had in the Christmas spirit felt like it had been ripped from her.

Finally finding her voice, she screamed, "This is bullshit!" She buried her head into the blankets and pillows she'd been buried under.

Barb, Dee, and Kate sat down and tried to console the weeping Ophelia, only just realizing this probably wasn't the best way to relay the message to her.

"Okay, girls . . . why don't you leave her alone. She's obviously not taking this one well," said Lillian as she came into the living room. Lillian always had a practical way of talking to her daughters.

Seeing the commotion from outside, Mickey, Chuck, and Jet came in from the backyard to find the women surrounding a weeping Ophelia.

Trenton, the only missing family member, was fast asleep in his room. He had already learned the truth about Santa years earlier and had fallen asleep after too many video games and one too many pieces of pie that evening.

"Well, I guess this didn't go too well, did it now, ladies?" said Chuck as he saw his little niece sobbing. "As usual, you all didn't think something through."

Mickey, seeing the heartbreak in his little girl, stepped in.

"All right, Barb. That's enough. I'll take it from here." He scooped up his tiny little daughter and carried her into her bedroom, placing her gently onto her bed. He sat down beside her, where he stayed until she fell back to sleep. He didn't say much. He never did when he saw Ophelia upset. Somehow Mickey always knew when words weren't needed, when the strength of his presence was enough. It wouldn't be the first time he took her away when he saw his daughter upset, and it certainly wouldn't be the last.

2

OPHELIA'S GRANDMOTHER

Ophelia looked at her grandmother's house, conflicting emotions roiling in her gut.

It hadn't always been like this. Just last year she would have had her seatbelt off before the car came to a stop, and she'd be bounding up her grandmother's front step before her mother killed the engine. What changed? Was it just part of growing up? *And learning people's secrets*, she realized.

That was it. Last year, she thought of her grandmother almost like a magical fairy who took her under her wing and made her dreams come true. She was the one who let Ophelia have ice cream for breakfast, the one who let her stay up late watching movies, the one who could be talked into a yes after her mother said no.

But she knew better now. Her grandmother was taking on a new dimension in her eyes. And Ophelia wasn't sure she liked it. She liked her magical fairy grandmother. What had started it? Maybe learning that Lillian had lived through the dire years of the Great Depression or hearing her aunts label their mother a "hoarder" or recognizing a sadness had crept into her grandmother's eyes that hadn't been there in all her pictures with Grandpa Carl.

Ophelia snapped out of her daze and managed to put on a big smile as her grandmother opened the car door. "Hey there, O! You made it," Lillian said cheerfully.

Reflexively, Ophelia met her eyes. Her stomach squeezed again as her grandmother's gaze confirmed Ophelia's thoughts. The familiar sadness was still there, despite the warmth in her voice.

"A long weekend with my favorite girl. Just the thing I've been wishing for," Lillian said. "Come on in, Princess. I have a treat waiting for you."

Ophelia's view of Lillian was made up of memories of her visits and the trips they took through her childhood. To Ophelia, Lillian was magical and complicated. She was the matriarch of the Harold women and oftentimes the center of their stories.

Born beautiful and intelligent, Lillian spent most of her life experiencing and recovering from great loss. It would take years for Ophelia to understand her, but as pieces to the puzzle came together, it all made sense as to why Lillian experienced the ups and downs of emotion that Ophelia saw her grandmother wear throughout her life. Lillian was two sides of the coin to Ophelia; on one side she would see her grandmother's zest for adventure, and on the other was her bitterness toward the world and all that had been taken from her. You'd never know which side you would get with Lillian on any given day. She had the passion to accomplish great things, but she didn't always have the motivation to actually complete them. Her life reflected a hurry-up-and-wait mentality.

Grandmothers are magical to little girls. They pass down their stories to them starting at a young age, telling them all their tales throughout their lives. But behind the tales there was a woman who carried deep sadness that Ophelia would see more and more of as the years progressed. Lillian had been through a lot in life, and Ophelia would only learn this more and more as she grew older.

Nevertheless, the love story of Carl and Lillian always inspired hope in Ophelia. As a young girl, she was certain every person had a perfect soul mate out there waiting for them and that everyone would have one great love in their life.

As the years passed and Ophelia grew into a young adult, she learned of the storms that her "fairy grand-mother" had weathered. And the pieces of the puzzle began to come together to tell her story. In her adult life, Ophelia learned life was all about learning to play the hand you were dealt. While no one ever expects a bad hand to be dealt us in life, it's how one learns to play that bad hand and move forward that shapes us and sets us on the path. Lillian had been dealt difficult hands in her life, and she'd been brave in surviving every one of those tragedies. It was something Ophelia came to admire in her as she grew into adult life.

Lillian always had her emotions together and rarely

showed her cards. She was built to be tough and rarely ever showed her sadness. The pain she felt came out disguised as bitterness.

Lillian was raised by a poor family on a small farm in rural West Texas during the Great Depression and World War II era. Like most people who lived through that era, the family always held on to everything they had, never taking one meal for granted. They were constantly trying to keep the family farm afloat, and Lillian's dad did all he could to support the family. But many times there was barely a meal to put on the table.

Her parents taught her to appreciate the little she was given, and she'd learned at a young age to work for what she had. Like most born in that generation, Lillian obsessed over collecting things, even food, and it was a habit that followed her all her life. You never knew where your next meal would come from—that's what the Depression years of limited work and starving families taught her.

Dee, Barb, Kate, and Ophelia labeled her a "hoarder," constantly taking turns throwing things away in Lillian's house, hoping she wouldn't notice. Lillian was one of the smartest women Ophelia knew. She was so smart that most of the time she couldn't articulate things into simple English for others to understand. She could write out and prove any scientific theory but could barely write a letter to a friend.

Lillian was naturally beautiful and extremely intelligent; she always had been. Like the other adult Harold women, she stood at an average height of five foot six and was slender with long, dark reddish-brown hair. She had pale skin that always looked like pristine porcelain, complemented by her long eyes that matched her slender face. She possessed a smile that would light up a room and a contagious laugh that could be heard a mile away. Ophelia often looked at photos of a young Lillian placed around the Harold home and was in awe of her grandmother's natural beauty.

Raised under her mother's strict rules, Lillian was rarely ever allowed off the farm except to attend school. Her mother was determined to raise a "lady" who would one day marry well. Lillian was expected to be a wife and run her own household. "Grandma Topher," as Barb, Dee, and Kate called her, raised Lillian to be a wife.

Barb and the aunts were fond of saying the woman "did not put up with any shit."

"That's one woman you never wanted to cross," Barb and the aunts always told O.

Grandma Topher expected Lillian to raise a family of her own and settle down with a nice, young man. She didn't care for Lillian's ambitions. She was tough on Lillian through her growing up years, but the mother-and-daughter pair had an enduring relationship that only made sense to them.

"She just had her set of rules, my darling." Lillian explained to Ophelia one afternoon over ice cream sandwiches. Ophelia had been spending the weekend at Lillian's, as she did every summer growing up. She and Lillian spent most of the afternoon going through old photos while Lillian told Ophelia about her family. "She wasn't a bad woman. I loved her very much. Just if you didn't follow her rules, well, hell, she was going to make you pay for it!" Lillian laughed.

Still, Lillian couldn't help her mother had held her back, despite the warmth between them. Lillian didn't have much interest in becoming someone's wife. O had never met Grandma Topher, as she'd pass long before Ophelia arrived into the world. But she'd heard stories of her growing up.

It was at school that Lillian felt most at home. Lillian spent most of her life buried in books, always desiring to learn more. Naturally very smart, she found school to be easy. Her favorite subjects were science and mathematics because she could get lost in numbers, equations, and scientific theories. Education was the great love of Lillian's life. She surrounded herself with books, usually reading two or three at a time. Her need to be informed and educated on every subject possible made her into a brilliant woman.

When she wasn't studying, Lillian found comfort in her only friend, her older sister Evelyn. The two of them imagined one day of running away from the ranch to pursue their own dreams and not their mother's. Evelyn was the one person Lillian could confide in. Many times at sunset, the sisters would take long walks, hand in hand, around the farm as they discussed their dreams and envisioned what their future lives held for them somewhere out there in the distance.

Evelyn, born just as beautiful as her younger sister, Lillian, aspired to be a movie star in the "pictures" as they called them back then. She had read of Hollywood and aspired to stand alongside the women she looked up to:

Katharine Hepburn and Vivien Leigh. She had a knack for drama and always saw herself becoming famous, dripping in jewels, and donning fur coats while attending Hollywood's best parties.

Lillian, on the other hand, dreamed of leaving the farm life to pursue higher education and of one day running a school on her own and passing down to others all she had learned. Lillian's heroes were Charles Darwin and Albert Einstein. She believed in science and theories that could be tested and proven to explain why the world was the way it was. Lillian never believed anything unless she had evidence to support it.

The two also talked endlessly of leaving the farm life behind to travel the world they had only read about. Lillian aspired to see all the natural wonders and beauty of the world. She hoped to one day stand on top of the Grand Canyon, explore the ancient Native American caves and homes, hike through Alaska, and explore Yellowstone National Park. Evelyn saw her travels taking her to Paris, Rome, and Monaco, where she would sip the finest champagne and eat the most delicious foods.

But Evelyn never made it to the "pictures," Ophelia would find out one day while playing in Lillian's bathroom. The eight-by-ten portrait of her sister sat on the vanity table next to her tray of perfume.

"Who's that, Lillian?" Ophelia asked, puzzled at the stranger staring back at her in the photo. Ophelia had called Lillian by her name since she was little. Barb and the aunts always had and she never knew it differently.

"My sister, Evelyn. She died young." Lillian kept her

answer short. Because of this, Ophelia would later ask Barb what had happened to Evelyn.

One morning while Lillian was getting ready for school, she walked into the bathroom she shared with Evelyn to find her sister dead in the bathtub. Evelyn suffered from epilepsy and had drowned while soaking in her bath that morning. She slipped away so quietly that no one, not even Lillian, could have saved her. She was just shy of her eighteenth birthday, and all the dreams the sisters had once shared were snatched from them. It was the first heartbreak Lillian had felt. She'd lost her best and only friend, the only person she felt she could talk to. As she watched her sister being laid to rest, she promised her she'd live and see the world for the both of them.

The young Evelyn was poised there in black and white, staring out from the heavy encrusted gold picture frame with a huge grin on her face. Evelyn would always be young and beautiful.

"She looks like a movie star!" a young O exclaimed as she grabbed the frame while watching Lillian do her makeup.

"She was very beautiful indeed, and she was taken away at too young of an age. She never got to experience anything in life," said Lillian as she got up from the chair, tightened her robe, and exited her makeup room.

That was all Ophelia could get out of her grandmother on the subject of her sister. She wasn't too surprised, though. Her grandmother usually kept her emotions to herself. *Is that another lesson learned early in the Depression years?* Ophelia wondered. Ophelia always saw a great amount of strength in her grandmother with how she held herself together.

Though Lillian never confirmed this, Ophelia was right. Lillian was raised to never show emotion because she was taught that it represented weakness. She buried everything deep within her.

She had been just shy of twenty when fate stepped in, when Dr. Carl Harold showed up and swept her off her feet. The young, up-and-coming orthopedic surgeon was immediately taken with Lillian the day their paths crossed at the local ice cream parlor in Lillian's small hometown.

Carl was tall and slender with dark hair and a strong personality; he prided himself on the fact that he didn't take shit from anyone. In no time at all, Carl fell in love with Lillian's natural beauty and large smile. And Lillian was enamored with the way people looked at Carl when he walked into a room with pride and confidence. Carl was on his way back to Abilene to begin his practice and was determined to take Lillian with him from the moment he laid eyes on her. They fell crazy in love and were married within two months of that first meeting.

Growing up in a wealthy family, Carl had a zest for the finer things in life. Lillian did her best to fit into Carl's lavish lifestyle, but, truth be told, she never cared about the money, the jewels he showered on her, or the luxurious life they lived. It was more about being with a man who loved and adored her.

Carl and Lillian would inherit his parents' beautiful home, which sat on five acres of land. The Harold home was the largest in Abilene at the time. Carl's parents had built the home in the early 1900s, sparing no expense to house many rooms for entertainment. It was more than enough for a young doctor and his wife, especially when they dreamed of filling it with a family of their own. Carl and Lillian later added on to the house, built a pool, and constructed a giant patio. A corner house, the place became an icon in the town and hosted many parties throughout the years.

In the early years, Dr. Carl Harold became known as one of the best orthopedic surgeons in West Texas. The patient wait list was always full, and people would travel from across the state to come have surgery performed by Dr. Carl Harold. He was brilliant, and he knew it. Lillian learned to become the perfect, picturesque wife of her brilliant surgeon husband, just as her mother had always intended her to be. She gave up her studies and much of her identity to partake in Carl's lifestyle and eventually raise their three girls.

Carl loved her dearly and showed it, showering Lillian with gifts and affection and taking her to every play and high-end restaurant in town. They often drove to Austin and Dallas to go to the symphony or attend charitable events. From the outside looking in, Lillian and Carl had a perfect marriage. Lillian was happy and proud of the man she stood behind.

"They had the type of love that you see in fairy tales. She was the damsel, living a life that was going nowhere, and he was the valiant prince who rode in to carry her away to a better life," Barb told Ophelia one night. Despite giving up her own dreams, Lillian's marriage to Carl gave her some of the happiest years of her life. She loved him for the brilliant man he was, for the way he looked at her with love in his eyes, and for the family he gave her. He ushered her into a life she'd never had, a life of comfort. But buried beneath that perfect marriage, Lillian felt many times that she was without a voice of her own.

"Carl believed that unless you had a PhD, you didn't know anything," Lillian told Ophelia later on in life. "I was only allowed to hang out with his friends because they were doctors or doctors' wives. I gave up a lot for that man, even some of my closest friends."

Carl was always a mystery to Ophelia growing up. On the one hand she'd hear of the great love of Lillian's life, and on the other he was the man who always held her back from becoming the woman she wanted to be.

But the only Dr. Carl Harold that Ophelia ever knew was a man in a wheelchair who could hardly speak. Over the years, Carl developed a severe drinking problem that only got worse as the years passed. When he wasn't at his practice or performing surgery, he was usually found drinking. He had gotten to the point in his life where he required a drink the moment he woke up in the morning.

As the years wore on, his drinking led to a vicious and bad attitude toward a lot of the couple's friendships. His reputation of the fun-loving surgeon would soon wane, and then he was known more frequently as a volatile drunk. Mickey once told Ophelia that in the later years of his life, Carl alienated most of his and Lillian's friends due to his drinking.

"It just got hard to be around him. You never knew what would come out of his mouth," Mickey explained to Ophelia one night while they were at dinner. Ophelia was approaching her thirties and struggling with ideas of marriage and long-term commitment. The older she got, the more she learned. Relationships she once viewed as perfect were showing what they really were. Ophelia didn't know this man who had been in the lives of Lillian, Barb, and the aunts.

"He'd get arrogant, and every other word out of his mouth was profanity. It wasn't any fun to be around him those last several years."

Ophelia was very young when Carl suffered the stroke that put him in a wheelchair and robbed him of many of his motor skills. He required constant care; he could barely feed himself or go to the bathroom on his own. Lillian spent the last remaining years of his life by his side, caring for him at the Harold home, while Dee, Barb, and Kate took turns rotating in visits to help their mother.

In the years that she cared for her husband, the once beautiful Lillian gained fifty pounds. The years weathered her, and her face betrayed the tireless long nights she nursed Carl. The once slender woman slipped away as taking care of herself was no longer a priority.

She watched the love of her life die slowly over the years. Widowed at fifty-five and with grown daughters starting their own lives and adventures, Lillian fought for strength every day to move on with her life. She just didn't know how to live without Carl; she didn't want to. Carl's death left a deep hole in Lillian's heart; it was a loss that was never repaired.

Ophelia always knew that her grandfather's passing put Lillian over the edge. But as Ophelia grew older and experienced loss in her own life, she understood Lillian much better. She was a brokenhearted woman who would live with longing for her soul mate for the rest of her life.

"Will you ever marry again?" Ophelia had once asked Lillian when she was young.

"Darling, I already had my great love story and spent the best years of my life with my soul mate. And there's no sense in ever moving on from that," explained Lillian.

After Carl's passing, Lillian would pick back up her dreams to achieve what she had always set out to do. She reclaimed her dreams of higher education she had put on hold when she married Carl.

Lillian went on to teach at the local Abilene college and earned her PhD in mathematics at age sixty. Ophelia was never more proud of Lillian than on the day she graduated with her PhD. And Lillian felt she had finally proved to Carl she was just as smart as he was by earning her title of "doctor" too. Ophelia always secretly wished she'd inherited her grandmother's brilliance. She couldn't tip a server properly without her iTip app on her iPhone.

Despite reaching her educational goal, Lillian slipped into depression after Carl's death. It was a depression that perhaps had been growing in her for a long time but didn't come into full effect until she watched the love of her life slowly slip away. The emotions she had tucked deep down in her for years all came to light as she entered a new era of her life, living on her own.

The path of loneliness was a dark one for Lillian. She kept a brave face, but days on end in solitude snuffed out her drive to do anything. She often felt her mind was running wild, and the pain of her loss only made her isolate herself further.

As the years pressed on, the once beautiful Harold home slowly began to fall apart. Lillian became what Ophelia would learn to be as a hoarder. The home that once held so many parties and memories became piled with junk over the years. The dining room stored every newspaper and magazine Lillian ever touched. Ophelia once found an old *Cosmopolitan* magazine issue from twenty years earlier in a stack of magazines when she visited Lillian during college. She'd spent the large part of her visit cleaning out the house. A weekend would only cover a small portion of what was needed to restore the Harold home back to its original charm. Ophelia also tried to tackle the landscaping that hadn't been touched in years but ended up with poison oak all over her instead.

O tried to throw the old magazine away, but Lillian wouldn't have it.

"Don't throw that away! I'm going to read that, Ophelia!" Lillian shouted as she motioned for Ophelia to withdraw her retreat to the trashcan with the magazine.

"You know the sex advice in here is probably really outdated by now. They've come up with much better stuff since then," Ophelia said sarcastically as she returned the magazine to the pile of newspapers that had been accumulating for years.

The cigar room where Grandfather once kept his pipes to smoke at night with his cup of brandy had become a museum of VHS tapes, CDs, and records collecting dust. The kitchen counters were almost always covered in mail that had piled up for weeks and months at a time. The refrigerators (there were several: one in the kitchen, one in the garage, and one in the common area leading to the pool) were full of food that had sat in there for months at a time. And the bottles of Coors Light probably dated back to Ophelia's birth. Trenton once tried to drink one, but immediately spat it out. Ophelia always compared the Harold home to the house of the crazy aunt in one of her favorite novels, *Great Expectations*. She'd tease that it'd be the perfect fit for the next episode of *Hoarders*.

When he died, Carl left behind a large sum of money for Lillian to inherit, hoping it would take care of her for the remainder of her life. Though he never intended to leave Lillian alone, he wanted to ensure she was taken care of.

Lillian spent the money on extravagant purchases and took Ophelia and Trenton on trips of a lifetime. Some of Ophelia's greatest adventures were during her teenage years, driving all over the western United States with Lillian during the summer months. They drove for days on end all over Texas, New Mexico, Arizona, Colorado, Utah, Idaho, and Wyoming, visiting all the natural wonders the Great West had to offer.

Lillian was determined to experience every national park with her two grandchildren. Ophelia and Trenton counted these as some of their best memories with their grandmother. One summer Lillian drove Trenton and Ophelia to Yellowstone National Park, where they spent an entire day waiting for Old Faithful to erupt. Every time they came back to see it, they missed it, but Lillian wouldn't let them leave until they saw it. After four attempts, they finally saw it, and all three agreed it was worth the drive.

In those years, Ophelia was too young to understand

money, but she was always curious how Lillian managed the funds that Grandfather had left behind. O never did find out how much it was. She always assumed it was a lot, though, because every trip they took together, Lillian spent as if there was no end of money in sight. It worried the rest of the family, but there was no stopping her.

"Lillian is a brilliant mathematician and can solve any equation, but the woman cannot balance a checkbook to save her life," Ophelia overheard Mickey saying to Barb one night.

One afternoon when Ophelia was thirteen, she and Lillian wandered the streets of Jackson Hole, Wyoming, together, arm and arm, when Lillian pulled Ophelia into a jewelry store. The store was filled with diamonds, gold, silver, rare sapphires, turquoise, emeralds, rubies, opals, and beyond. Lillian's eyes lit up, mesmerized by the jewelry; she was a kid in a candy store.

Ophelia would never forget how Lillian fell in love with a gold necklace and matching earrings that had a hand-carved scene of an elk walking through the Grand Tetons. As the jeweler spoke of the local artist, Lillian only became more enamored with the piece of gold. Of course as the jeweler presented it, she told Lillian it was one of a kind, which only persuaded Lillian more. The necklace and earrings retailed at $10,000, and Lillian barely blinked when the saleswoman read her the price.

"What do you think, O? Isn't it beautiful? Should I get it?" asked Lillian.

"Sure," shrugged Ophelia. At thirteen, Ophelia didn't have a concept of money, nor did she know exactly Lillian's worth. But she did know it was an extreme amount of money to spend on an elk necklace. Lillian handed the saleswoman her credit card, and the jewelry was hers.

Ophelia never did grow to understand these types of purchases. Lillian only wore the necklace once in her entire life. These extravagant purchases slowly drained all that was left of the Harold money.

Ophelia never was an admirer of jewelry like her grandmother, and maybe this was why. She watched purchases like this drain the funds Carl had left for Lillian. Ophelia also never saw the point in spending an extreme amount of money on something so small and simple.

As Ophelia and Trenton entered their adult years, their adventures with Lillian ended. Lillian's money had run out, and Trenton and Ophelia were busy navigating their adult lives. The loneliness and the thought of no new adventure to look forward to made Lillian sink deeper into her depression.

Eventually Dee, Barb, and Kate urged Lillian to sell the Harold home as it slipped into disarray and her wealth disappeared. At least there was still great value in the land. The home that Lillian and Carl had hoped to keep in the family and pass down to one of their daughters or grandchildren was put on the market. Barb came to clean out and rid the house of most of Lillian's things, everything she'd so carefully hoarded over the years. Lillian yelled at Barb, watching helplessly at all the items she tossed away.

The giant Harold home sold, only to be bulldozed to the ground. What was left of Lillian's things were packed up in a small U-Haul. She moved in with Dee and Chuck and spent her days watching Fox News, reading books, and completing crossword puzzles from the newspaper.

She rarely left the house, and her health declined. She had lost all lust for life. Neglecting her health made it much more difficult for Lillian to get around, and she felt as if her life was coming to an end. When anyone asked Lillian how she was doing or if they could take her on any trip, she refused to leave her chair. She wasn't shy about admitting "I'm ready to die."

3

THE HAROLD DAUGHTERS OR BARB
AND THE AUNTS

I raised them the best I knew how, she thought as she stared into the cluttered room of hers surrounded by books. Lillian had barely left her room in weeks. She looked down at her hands . . . wrinkled and tired. She was in her seventies now. She never thought she'd live to be this old and certainly didn't think she'd live this long without Carl. Barb and Kate were not talking again. She didn't understand why those two could never get along. *You would think they could just be happy for each other. But I guess I did this to them, or maybe just their paths of life did.*

In her early years, Lillian was determined to raise her three daughters to be strong and independent. She would teach Dee, Barb, and Kate to forge their own paths without the need for any man to take care of them. Lillian taught her daughters worth and intelligence, always weighing that to be more important than beauty. All three were uniquely different, and each had a mind of her own. Raised to be West Texas debutantes, they grew up privileged, yet hardworking and independent. The adoration for the two parents who raised them was the only thing they shared in common. They each grew to lead very different lives.

Barb: the brains, the horsewoman, the one determined to have it all.

Gripping the reins tighter and leaning farther forward, she gave her painted horse, Willow, a little kick to pick up the speed. Her long hair whipped wildly in the wind. Barb was flying on the back of Willow as they sprinted across the field at full speed. It was in the field behind the Harold house on the back of Willow where Barb spent most days growing up. This was her escape from reality, the place she felt most free. Her connection to the soul in a horse brought her peace. It was a "bug" she caught early on. Horses would always be her first love.

Barb first fell in love with horses when she attended a local rodeo. It was the way they moved, their smell, the power and strength they embodied, and how fast they ran. They were free spirits. A horsewoman's connection to horses was said to be a very powerful connection. They connected through the eyes and were bonded for life.

Barb longed to have her own horse from a young age. After finding his daughter asleep many nights in the stables, Carl bought Barb her first horse, Willow. It was the greatest gift her parents ever gave her, and every day Barb rode him through the fields.

In high school, Barb became a barrel racer in the local rodeos. She had a competitive nature—always had to be the best at everything. She won almost every rodeo she ever attended. But on the days she wasn't competing and she just needed to escape her adolescent life, she found herself climbing on Willow's back to run through the fields behind the Harold home for miles and miles until they were both out of breath.

As the middle sister, Barb always felt the need to be the center of attention. She stood at an average height and was very thin. She had blue-green eyes that were perfectly blended together. Her hair was dark reddish-brown, long, and thick, and her smile was so large it lit up a room. Her perfect skin was almost always undisturbed by any blemish. She possessed true natural beauty, so much so that even as she grew older, it was hard to guess her true age.

Barb's voice and laughter could be heard from miles away. You always knew when she entered the room. Barb made damn sure people knew she was there. It was her loud behavior that often bothered Ophelia in her adolescent years, but as she grew older, Ophelia learned to appreciate her mother's need to be heard.

Despite her natural beauty, Barb was unconcerned with her appearance and rarely spent time on herself. She always knew she was beautiful, but it never defined who she was. She cared more about intelligence, culture, and heart. Like Lillian, she had a great love of books, and when she wasn't on the back of a horse, she had her nose in a book. She looked up to Jane Austen, William Shakespeare, and Charles Dickens. Their works allowed her to escape into another world, a world where she dreamed of seeing many great places and finding true love.

Growing up as the middle child, Barb always felt entitled to run the family. She relentlessly bossed her sisters around. She was the most outwardly emotional of the three, and the world seemed to constantly revolve around her. Everyone knew Barb wore her heart on her sleeve.

She strived for a level of perfection that often made Dee and Kate roll their eyes. Barb was never afraid to use her voice. She knew what she wanted, and she fought to have it. She dreamed of so much the world had to offer her. She knew she was cut out for bigger and greater things. She dreamed of Paris, of sitting outside and eating fresh croissants with an espresso in hand as she watched the people pass her by on the streets. She dreamed of traveling to other faraway places. And she dreamed of a man who would love her fiercely for who she was, but who would also let her be the free, independent, strong woman she wanted to be. She longed to run her own successful business in New York City and be on top of the world. She knew she'd be the most successful of her sisters and was determined to make her dreams come true. Barb had to have it all.

It was at the University of Texas where she first laid eyes on Mickey—at the annual rush parties in Austin on a hot summer day in August. Barb was a sophomore, attending with her fellow sorority sisters. Mickey was unloading kegs of beer the moment she first set her sights on him. Barb and Mickey locked eyes all night, but each was too timid to approach the other.

Mickey, a handsome, young central Texas farm boy, had all the appeal Barb was looking for. Polite, smart, and witty, Mickey was the guy everyone wanted to be around.

Everyone loved him. Every guy wanted to be his friend, and every girl wanted to date him.

A frat boy and Silver Spur for the University of Texas, Mickey knew everyone because of his kind and friendly attitude. He worked his way through college delivering Coors Light kegs to every frat party in Austin. He was the all-American blond boy with the contagious smile. Like Barb, Mickey was ambitious with big dreams. He saw himself running his own oil company in Texas one day.

It wasn't until the wee hours of the morning, when the party was winding down, that they first spoke to each other. Barb, who'd had one too many beers, was stumbling to get into her car with her friends when one of them accidentally ran over Barb's foot. She screamed so loudly she caused a scene. Mickey, not far away in the parking lot, ran to Barb's rescue. The problem was, he was still holding a very full keg of beer in both his hands. In a panic, he dropped the full keg of beer directly onto his foot. Hobbling in pain, Mickey stumbled over to rescue a crying Barb, only to call a cab to take them both to an emergency room.

Together in the Austin emergency room, Barb and Mickey learned they had both fractured their left foot. After being discharged, the two stumbled out into the parking lot, where the sun was rising. They locked eyes once again. Mickey leaned down and kissed Barb for the first time. Barb felt the world stop. Her fate was sealed; she knew she would marry this man. They walked from the parking lot hand in hand, the debutant from Abilene and the farm boy from central Texas, only to be joined in marriage two years later after graduating college.

After the wedding, they moved to Dallas to start their own businesses. Mickey set out to do what he was born to do—build his own oil business and make his name known in the great state of Texas. He set out to prove to everyone that a small farm boy from central Texas could make it.

Barb, determined to start a successful business of her own, would be no housewife. She struggled to build her ad agency in Texas. Her dreams of moving to New York to be in the advertising world ended the day she chose to marry Mickey. She eventually built a solid business she should have been proud of, but it never reached the success she always craved. Mickey never had any desire to leave Texas. He was a Texas boy, born and bred, and he'd be there till his last breath. Therefore, Barb set out to build the perfect life in Dallas. The couple had two children, Trenton and Ophelia. Mickey and Barb pooled all their money to buy a house on one of the most expensive streets in Dallas, where they dreamed of raising their family and building the life they'd always wanted.

Barb and Mickey settled into a predictable rhythm, but as they grew, they found less and less in common, and the spark of love they once shared began to fade in those first several years of marriage. They woke one day to find themselves in a loveless marriage, the fire of their love burned out. And they both changed as the years went on.

Barb still longed to run away and to travel the world, but Mickey never shared her dreams. She found refuge on the weekends riding the two thoroughbred horses she had proudly bought for herself. And most nights after her children were asleep, she poured herself a drink.

Her relationships with her children developed into two

different paths. Her bond with Trenton grew strong; Trenton admired the fight in his mother, and Barb felt the need to shield her son, no matter how much trouble he got into over the years. But her relationship with Ophelia was different, fading with time for reasons she never fully understood.

Some nights after a long day at the office and a long night riding her two horses, Barb would come home to find O playing in her playroom, and she just stared at her, longing for a connection with her daughter. While she saw so much of herself in O, she couldn't quite make a connection with her. More than once, she dragged O kicking and screaming from school and out to the horse stables. Her interests were just different from her daughter's. O never took pleasure in the riding lessons Barb arranged for her. Instead, she was more drawn to gymnastics and soccer.

The years took their toll on Barb, and she became more fragile with each year that passed and every inch that grew between her and Mickey. They'd become two business partners running a household.

Barb's drinking worsened over the years, and Dee came over and spent many nights in the backyard sharing wine while Barb cried on her shoulder. She fell into a depression that only seemed to grow with time. And it deepened as her dreams of traveling slipped further away, her marriage continued to fall apart, and O drifted further from her grasp. Despite it all, Barb never gave up hope. That was the fighter in her.

· · ·

DeeAnna "Dee": the comic relief, the animal lover, the steady heart

The eldest of the Harold sisters, DeeAnna, grew up the free spirit and was the calm one of the three sisters. Though she was the oldest, it was often Barb and Kate who ended up taking the lead. She set out to live a simple life, never craving the success her two sisters longed for. There wasn't much Dee had interest in other than attending the next party or hanging out with her closest friends.

Dee was slender just like Barb, though she had frizzy hair and buckteeth, which Carl and Lillian paid a large sum of money to have fixed when she was a teenager. Dee did not possess the same beauty that her two sisters were blessed with, but she definitely brought the most amount of entertainment. Her humor and wit made people want to be around her. She was a natural best friend and someone all different types of people were drawn to. She also had one of the biggest hearts Ophelia had ever seen, always taking care of those around her and never daring to judge anyone.

As the typical child of the sixties, Dee grew up a hippie. She was always mixed up with the party crowd, looking to have a good time, smoke a joint, and listen to good music. She didn't care for success. She cared more about being around those she could have a good time with. She started drinking early, a habit that worsened as she grew older, and she was a constant chimney of cigarettes.

Naturally smart, Dee became an accountant for a gas pipeline company and lived an average life. She met

Chuck, who was ten years older and divorced with kids of his own, though he never spoke to them anymore. She'd dated off and on, but she never met someone she felt connected to until the day Chuck walked into her life. Chuck accepted, understood, and loved Dee for the woman she was. He never wanted to change a thing about her. They lived a simple life together, mostly drinking their nights away with their many friends. Their house was always filled with people.

Dee and Chuck had a stable and happy marriage, for the most part. They loved each other deeply, but they always had a funny way of showing it, constantly making fun of each other. Ophelia never knew how two people could insult one other as much as they did and still look at each other with adoring eyes.

Their life made sense to them, and neither expected much of the other. Ophelia just figured it worked and they were happy living life together with their four dogs and four cats. Dee never wanted children, and Chuck had no desire to have more. Their animals were their children. Their home together looked like an episode from Animal Planet; you could find an animal in every room of the house. There were urine stains on the carpets and cat condos in the bedroom. Their house smelled of litter boxes and cigarette smoke. Though their house was always entertaining, guests couldn't leave without being covered in dog hair and slobber.

Trenton and Ophelia always loved to go to Dee and Chuck's house because there were no rules. They'd have Hamburger Helper for dinner because that was all Dee knew how to make, and they usually watched any R-rated movie they wanted. Ophelia also learned the "F word" at a very young age from Aunt Dee and discovered how to use it as a noun, verb, adjective, and adverb.

Dee had met Chuck's children when they were first married, but neither ever saw them again. Ophelia never knew them, and she wasn't allowed to bring them up in conversation, as they no longer spoke to their father. Dee was fine never having children. Trenton and Ophelia would be her "kids," second only to her dogs and cats.

The beauty of Dee was within. She felt everything. She could feel happiness, sense the pain in her sisters and mother, and always longed to bring peace to everyone's lives. Whenever someone wasn't getting along, it was always Dee trying to patch things up. She hated seeing others suffer, and all she ever wanted was for everyone to have a good time. She was there for the people she loved. But as the years passed, it was Dee everyone needed to be watching over.

Kate: the strong and graceful one

Born graceful and elegant and the youngest of the Harold sisters, Kate was the prima ballerina and claimed the crown of princess at an early age. Kate was bold and beautiful with a powerful head on her shoulders and a mind of her own. She stood at the same average height as her two sisters. Kate was built more like an athlete, more toned and fit than Dee and Barb, who were skin and bones. Kate inherited her mother's thick, reddish-brown hair and those light green eyes; that a person could get lost staring into them.

Dance was the love of Kate's life from a very early age. She dedicated herself to ballet in a way that displayed her persistence in accomplishing her goals on her own and her ability to rely on herself for everything. The larger age gap between Barb and Kate (unlike Dee and Barb, who were only two years apart), left Kate feeling like she trailed behind her oldest sister. But it also taught her to stand on her own two feet at an early age.

Growing up in Abilene, Texas, Kate was regarded as the beauty of the town, and every boy begged to date her. She was crowned homecoming queen and was easily the most popular girl in school. She was always surrounded by a large group of friends, though she preferred the company of just the few she trusted. Like Barb, Kate longed to leave her life in Texas behind to start a new one. Kate imagined herself as the Sugar Plum Fairy in *The Nutcracker*, performing at the San Francisco ballet and leaving behind everything she knew.

Kate followed in her father and sister's footsteps, attending the University of Texas. Naturally, Kate joined a sorority and had a large group of friends. She majored in advertising just like Barb. And she found herself spending most of her time with a boy named Harry. The Harold family was quick to nickname him "The Big Toe" for reasons Ophelia never understood. Kate's dreams of moving to San Francisco were put on hold when she accepted Harry's marriage proposal right after graduation. She accepted because that was what she thought she was supposed to do—get married in a grand wedding, settle down, and have a family. Deep down, though, she knew she did not love Harry.

Kate knew the marriage was a complete mistake on the rehearsal dinner night when she looked at Harry laughing and joking with his friends. It was then she had a glimpse of the rest of her life: she'd be Mrs. Big Toe living in some small town in Texas. She would be a wife and nothing more. Kate died inside just thinking about it. But the wedding festivities continued on.

"Kate! Harry sent you something!" Dee yelled as she came carrying a giant package to Kate.

Dee, Barb, and the rest of Kate's closest friends were all gathered around her in her room at the Harold home the night before her wedding. The group of women sat in Kate's giant bedroom on the hardwood floors, excited to see what Harry had sent.

The package was extremely heavy, so Kate placed it right between her legs and ripped into the paper.

"Oh dear God, is that a joke?" Barb said.

There it was, Harry's wedding present to Kate: a foot-tall marble statue of a frowning clown holding three balloons. Kate stared at it, looked at her friends, and asked them to pass the champagne. She shoved the statue aside. Kate cried herself to sleep that night before her wedding.

The next morning she woke on her wedding day to her father, Carl, standing at the foot of her bed.

"Princess, you don't have to do this. We're all behind you if you want to back out now," he said and grabbed her hand. He knew this wasn't the man for his youngest daughter. "I don't care about the money or how much this will cost me. This is your life, and you don't have to go through with this."

Kate sat up and gave her father a stone-cold look. "No, we've got a wedding to get to, Daddy."

At the age of twenty-one, Kate married "The Big Toe" that night at the church in Abilene where she'd grown up. She stood humiliated in front of all the Harold family's closest friends.

Not even eight months later, Kate slapped Harry with divorce papers. She packed up her things, took a sales job, and joined Dee and Barb in Dallas. She moved into a small house, perfect for her, and set her mind toward building a career. Love was not on her mind, and it took a backseat in her life for many years to come.

The clown statue lived on the floor of Barb and Mickey's laundry room next to the cat litter box for the next eighteen years. Ophelia never met Harry, as he and Kate were over and done before Ophelia was even born. But she always thought of him every time Barb told her to go clean the cat litter box in the laundry room.

That was how she thought of The Big Toe.

4

THE HAROLD FEMALE DYNAMIC

Ophelia took notice early on of the dynamic between Lillian, Dee, Barb, Kate, and herself. They were five related women, each with their own attitudes, opinions, and unique outlook on life. Though they rarely agreed on much, their deep emotional sensitivity toward life and each other bound them together. They all had the ability to feel deeply, though they expressed it differently. The tornados of emotion often put them at odds with one another.

At almost any point in time, at least two, if not all, of the women were in conflict with one another. Maybe it was like five alpha dogs trying to win a dog fight. Maybe it was that each was unwilling to yield their viewpoint on how life should be lived. Or maybe it was just their own insecurity that kept them at a constant longing for something more.

Ophelia felt Lillian loved each of her daughters equally. But Barb and the aunts disagreed. Dee, Barb, and

Kate bickered constantly, thinking that one or the other was getting more attention from their parents or was more highly favored. Ophelia always admired the relationship Lillian nurtured with each of her three daughters. Not one of their relationships was the same. In O's eyes, Lillian never played favorites. She'd raised three strong, successful daughters, who were not afraid to speak their minds. Lillian wanted it that way, having felt for so much of her life that she was without her own voice.

The dynamic between Barb and her sisters drove most of the drama in the family. Raised to speak their minds, the three never held back on expressing how they felt. Creating conflict was their expertise; resolving conflict was forever a challenge. They swept their disagreements under the rug and moved on, never fully healing the rifts that formed between them.

Barb and Kate never truly learned to get along—not even as children. Instead of accepting their differences, the two women used them against each other. Neither bothered trying to understand the other's point of view. Barb always felt that Kate was crazy and ran away from everything life threw at her. Kate always thought Barb was a nutjob.

Dee and Barb, on the other hand, had a natural bond that made them best friends. Dee sided with Barb in most situations. Barb barely listened to anyone, but she occasionally made exceptions for Dee. Though Dee and Barb had the closer bond, Dee never forgot about Kate and found herself in the middle of her sisters, trying to form a peace treaty between their opposing sides.

The one thing Lillian never did was get in the middle of her daughters' conflicts. She always let them fight it out, remaining a loyal mother to each daughter, never showing partiality.

As the middle child, Barb grew up with a sense of pride. She was determined to stand out and be better than Dee and Kate. Dee couldn't give two shits what Barb was to become. But Barb's attitude put a rift between her and Kate.

Over the years, Barb and Kate never quite saw eye to eye. Ophelia figured it was just because oil and vinegar don't mix. But was there something more deeply rooted at work? Left behind by Dee and Barb, Kate often felt excluded by her two sisters at a young age. Maybe it was the fact that the two were such strong personalities growing up under the same roof, or maybe it was that both were determined to rise above the other. Whatever the reason, Barb and Kate started off on the wrong foot and never managed to make things right between them.

Ophelia always felt the strain on their relationships was driven by jealousy. One always had something the other one lacked. It seemed they would be forever at odds.

"As long as I've known those women, Barb and Kate have never gotten along," Mickey told Ophelia as an adult.

Dee usually stayed out of the drama, but she sometimes found herself dragged into the middle of it as time went on. Barb had a flare for the dramatic and was always making mountains out of molehills. Dee most of the time found herself siding with Barb, which left Kate behind again, a painful reminder of their childhood dynamic.

It didn't help that Dee and Barb ganged up on Kate as kids too. Ophelia knew all too well the infamous story of the bathtub and dog piss. One Saturday morning the girls were all at the Harold home. Lillian was in the kitchen with symphony music blaring so loud she had tuned out Barb and Dee, who were running around the house chasing the family dog. Dee and Barb noticed the dog had managed to pee right at the bottom of the stairs. Rather than clean it up, the pair found this the perfect opportunity to plan their attack on Kate.

Kate was upstairs in the bathtub. Knowing her sisters were always up to something, she locked the door so that Barb and Dee could not get in. Dee and Barb, in their first attempt, tried to knock down the door.

"You can't get in here!" yelled young Kate, soaking in the bathtub. She giggled to herself, thinking she was safe by shutting the two of them out. Dee and Barb laughed to themselves outside the door; they weren't going to let a locked door stop them. Dee ran off only to return with a small pair of scissors. The resourceful girls used the shears to jimmy the lock. As soon as the lock was free, the door swung open.

Kate sat there naked and wide-eyed with horror at the sight of her sisters. Dee grabbed her legs while Barb grabbed her arms, and they hoisted Kate out of the tub. They carried a soaking-wet Kate down the stairs all the way down to the bottom, right where the dog had left a nice, large pool of urine. Dee and Barb dragged Kate's naked body right through the puddle as she screamed in rage.

"Oh, hell, what are you girls up to now?" screamed Lillian.

Their mother came out to the entryway to find Kate naked, crying, and pointing the finger at her two older sisters.

"Look at what they did, Mom!" yelled a hysterical Kate.

Lillian looked between the three girls, her two oldest huddled in the corner laughing hysterically.

"All right. You're just fine. Now get up and get upstairs and wash that off of ya," said Lillian. She said nothing else, just leaving the room shaking her head.

Despite their differences, though, the sisters managed to be there for one another, held together by the bonds of family. They nursed one another through love, heartbreak, marriage, and divorce. They never agreed on much or understood the life choices the others made, but they always found a way to support one another through large life events. They all loved Lillian and took turns caring for her as she aged. At different times, they each grew frustrated with her giving up on life, and they turned to one another to express their frustration. In the end they understood what she'd been through and grew to let her be.

The deep-rooted depression that Lillian carried trickled down to all three of her daughters. It was a mood disorder that each Harold woman carried and lived with. The Harold women were deeply affected by the highs and lows of their lives. The lows were the most difficult; each woman took tragedy so personally. They all questioned at one time or another, "Why did life turn out this way for me?" Each, in turn, learned the lesson that life is never what you pictured it to be when you were young and imaging the adult life you would have one day. Each had to find her own journey to happiness and contentment.

Ophelia always believed that the Harold women felt things more strongly than most people. They knew how to have the best of times, but when their hearts broke, it was like an earthquake with ripple effects. Getting over things and moving forward was something they struggled with. It was so easy to slip into a tunnel of darkness, to feel as if there was no way out. It was easy to feel as if the universe was against you. It was a disorder they all shared, and it tore them apart at times, made them frustrated with the others—but it also bonded them together.

The day Barb brought Ophelia into the world, a new Harold female entered the group. Barb and her sisters ("the aunts," as O referred to them) would fall instantly in love with the little one. Dee and Kate had already become aunts the day Trenton came into the world, but it was with the birth of Barb's daughter they felt a greater need to protect Ophelia. Knowing she was just like them, they understood she was born with a heart that would feel everything. They saw her fragility and knew if her heart was not protected properly, it would break easily.

Though the women prayed the depression that sat in all of them would not be passed down to their sweet princess, they felt deep down that one day it would be inevitable. They made a promise to themselves on Ophelia's birthday that they would always protect her. Ophelia was blessed that each of these women was placed in her life to not only look after her, but to raise her to be the strong woman they knew she was destined to be.

Not only had the aunts cast their shield over her, but Ophelia had a father and brother who had sworn to protect her for life. Ophelia was the apple of Mickey's eye. He'd fallen in love with her the instant she came into the world. Barb's quick labor had brought Ophelia charging into the world at full speed. She'd come so fast that the doctor barely made it in time to deliver her on that hot summer day in July. Mickey was there to pull Barb through and welcome his youngest and only daughter into the world. And Trenton, only three years old, met and fell in love with his little sister just as easily as his father had.

"You're the older brother now, Trenton. This is your little sister. You must look after her from this day forward," Mickey told him.

Trenton nodded as he looked down at her. Even at three, he knew this was his job.

The aunts filed in next to meet the newest and youngest member of the family.

"You know she kind of looks like Yoda," Dee said.

The whole family laughed. She did. Ophelia wasn't the best-looking baby, but there was a depth in her bright brown eyes as she stared back at her loving family.

"We were a little nervous when you first came out because you weren't the best-looking newborn. But boy when you hit two years old, you turned into one cute kid," Mickey told Ophelia. Ophelia always laughed at the thought of Dee comparing her to the Jedi master, Yoda. She giggled every time Dee told her the story.

As she got older, Ophelia grew into her beauty. She

inherited not only the emotional traits shared by the Harold women, but their physical attributes too. From Mickey, she gained resilience and calm. But on top of it all, she inherited the Harold women's deep emotional feelings, and she spent her life trying to understand what it all meant.

Though their shared depression so often felt like a curse, in a way it made them understand each other. Sometimes it felt it was the only ground from which they could relate to one other.

The depression was passed on to Ophelia, and it was Ophelia's biggest battle in her adult years. Even still, it couldn't match the degree of Lillian's depression; of all the Harold women, Lillian possessed the greatest amount of their shared darkness. Though the women couldn't escape this shadowed bond, they each chose their own path through it.

Lillian denied it and let it grow.

Dee found alternative methods to deal with it.

Barb and Kate embraced it, enjoying the antidepressants that came with it.

And Ophelia? She was determined to face it, fight it, and overcome it.

5

OPHELIA GROWING UP

G rowing up, a child always believes she has an ordinary childhood and a normal family life. It wasn't until Ophelia's adult years that she realized her childhood was anything but normal.

Mickey and Barb raised Trenton and Ophelia in a privileged environment. They provided for their children's every need while also keeping them grounded and ensuring they understood how to work hard. They lived a nice life in Dallas. Dee and Chuck and Kate lived close by.

But it was true that Ophelia and Trenton were spoiled rotten for years by their parents and two aunts. Ophelia led a happy childhood, surrounded by a loving family and attending school with lots of friends. Ophelia found herself involved in ballet, gymnastics, soccer, and baseball, anything that would keep her active. She loved the outdoors and playing with her friends. When she wasn't at school or practice, she had many sleepovers at Aunt Dee's or Aunt Kate's house, depending on whose turn it was.

Trenton and Ophelia loved their time with their aunts. Dee and Kate treated their niece and nephew as if they were their own children.

Barb and Mickey's house often hosted Dee, Chuck, and Kate for dinner. Mickey and Chuck spent their time on the back porch, while Barb and the aunts were always in the kitchen together. Ophelia noticed early on how much the women in her family drank. It was almost a ritual to sit around and discuss life over several glasses of wine. Although she didn't fully understand the effects of the alcohol, she'd seen them doing a lot of it. Did this have anything to do with the way many nights ended in arguments between the sisters?

Most of the time, though, O lapsed into her own dream world. She was mesmerized by the fairy tale stories of Cinderella and Sleeping Beauty. She dreamed of meeting her own prince one day. It made her believe in love and chivalry and in the possibility of her own happily ever after. This was a feeling she carried with her through the years, the expectation of this fairy tale future and the man who would whisk her away to her eternal happiness.

Dee showed Ophelia *Pretty Woman* at a young age because it was her favorite movie. Like Ophelia, Dee also believed in true love stories. It probably was not the best movie to show a young girl, even though it would be years before Ophelia realized that Vivian was a prostitute Edward picked up off Hollywood Boulevard. All Ophelia saw was the love story. She waltzed into the kitchen one night after watching *Pretty Woman* in Dee's living room for the tenth time and announced to Barb and the aunts that she wanted to marry Richard Gere.

"And why is that?" Barb asked, chuckling over her glass of chardonnay.

"Because he takes you to nice hotels and buys you nice things," said a young Ophelia.

Dee, Barb, and Kate all laughed.

"Oh boy, Barb! Wait till Lillian hears about this. Only our princess!" said Dee.

Ophelia always dreamed of whom she would be when she grew up, and she couldn't wait to get there. She saw herself as a strong, self-sufficient woman, just like the women raising her. She'd bypass her entire childhood if she could just to be the woman she imagined herself to be. With the world at her fingertips, she'd be fully alive, happy, and healthy. She'd make her impact on the world. She knew she was destined to do great things.

And Ophelia dreamed of *him*. Even at a very young age, she dreamt of the prince who would one day save her and ride by her side. He'd be kind, funny, and handsome. And he'd love and adore the woman she was. In return, she would give him her heart and love him with all she had. He'd take her in his arms and keep her next to his heart forever. It was a love story she knew she was born to have. She was meant to be on this planet to love another.

As the years passed, Barb's kids watched their aunts forge their own paths, and their nights together became distant childhood memories. Kate announced one day that she was taking a job in San Francisco. Her life in Dallas was at a standstill, and she simply couldn't take another day of it. She had been offered a career opportunity that she couldn't turn down, one that promised to catapult her into a successful career. She left behind her life and her family in Texas. She felt lost watching everyone move on with their lives except her. It was her time to start her own journey, even if it meant going down the path alone.

Dee settled into her routine. Dee and Chuck both worked every day and came home to a house full of dogs and cats and wine and cigarettes. Dee and Chuck's life was simple, but they were rich in friends. They spent many nights laughing in their kitchen with those they adored. Those were always the happiest times in Dee's life.

Barb and Mickey's marriage grew stale as each year passed, but they kept a brave face for their children. Barb built and ran her business by day, struggling to keep it afloat, and rode horses by night and on weekends. Mickey spent more and more time away, building success year after year.

This brand of family life felt normal to Ophelia; she had never known it any other way. And for a long time, she was happy. But with adolescence came the rush of feelings and experiences that just overwhelmed her. Her eyes were opened to the outside world, and she found herself looking inward at all that was happening.

Despite the uncertainty in her world, Ophelia remained a dreamer. She always believed she was capable of anything and knew she'd one day live a successful life. With parents like Barb and Mickey, who were building businesses of their own, she was bound to succeed. Barb saw the potential in Ophelia and knew her daughter was capable of great things. But so much of her focus on her daughter was about conforming her to the way she thought things should be or how she should view the world.

Though Barb felt a mother and daughter should share a special connection, she struggled to bond with her daughter from early on. Barb spent many years trying to make things right, but somehow she never knew exactly what O needed. She was always pushing too hard for a solution instead of sitting back to let O be the woman she needed to grow into. She couldn't relax into being the strong, supportive woman Ophelia needed in her life.

Ophelia needed a strong woman to look up to. She saw the strength Barb had to be a successful, smart woman, but she was also privy to Barb's emotional outbursts and temper. It seemed there was always something going wrong in her mother's life. There was always someone to be angry with or another tear to shed. She'd seen her mother crying on Dee's shoulder too many nights to count.

At the time, Ophelia didn't know what it was about. Maybe it was her marriage falling apart. Or maybe it was that she had gone down a path she hadn't pictured for herself. But Ophelia learned the word *depression* very early in life. It seemed to be the dark cloud always lurking in the corner. It took Ophelia years to learn that Barb couldn't control her emotions or her disregard for how they affected those around her.

Ophelia's household with two loving parents was also a household of two separate people running things differently. Mickey was buried in work to build a life for himself and his family. Barb worked to become the successful advertising executive she always dreamed of, still working toward becoming the horse jumping champion of Texas. Her hobby and her work life took up the bulk of her time, and still she strived to maintain her home life. She constantly struggled to do it all. It was never enough for Barb. Ophelia always admired how she juggled everything, but sometimes she just wished for a friend.

Ophelia attended the private school that Mickey and Barb had worked so hard to send her and Trenton to. Barb was building the picturesque life for her family on the outside. Dee and Kate never cared for the materialistic life like Barb did. They only cared about living normal, comfortable lives.

"I hope to one day stand from my house looking down at all the peasants beneath me," Barb said one night, half joking to her sisters after one too many glasses of wine.

Dee was on her tenth cigarette of the night, and Kate really had just come over scrounging for leftover food from the dinner that Mickey had prepared earlier for the kids.

Dee rolled her eyes but didn't let Barb's comment faze her. Whatever Barb wanted was what Barb wanted; frankly, Dee just cared that Barb was happy. Kate, on the other hand, was completely disgusted by her sister's comment. It reminded her of the life she was trying to escape from.

Ophelia made friends easily at school. Her friendly, calm attitude always drew people to her. Making friends was never a challenge for Ophelia. Boys liked her, even at a young age. Ophelia was a beautiful little girl, but she had a tomboy streak to her too. She loved to play soccer at recess and beat the boys instead of playing house on the playground with the other girls.

In the environment of their small private school, mothers were overly involved with their children. Most days, the mothers came up to school to bring their children lunch, or they were there first thing in the morning, running the bake sale or selling tickets for the school fair that week. This was the type of mom Barb always said she wasn't going to be. Barb was determined to have a life of her own, separate from her family life to keep the balance.

Ophelia was heartbroken, though, every time Barb failed to show up. She always secretly hoped that maybe one day her mom would be there participating just like the other moms did. At such a young age, she didn't understand her mother had other major responsibilities in her life. All she knew was she had to scavenge to pack a decent lunch on her own while everyone else's mother either packed them a lunch or hand-delivered it to them.

Ophelia made a pact with herself that she would one day do it all if she ever had a child. She'd make all the sacrifices necessary to do everything for her child, to be the kind of mother she wished for herself. She'd be the best of the best in her career, and she'd be there for every moment in her child's life—no matter what it took.

Barb made her own way to spend time with Ophelia. She'd try to get Ophelia into horseback riding. She took Ophelia out to the stables many nights, many times against Ophelia's will—horses never interested O. While most children spent their afternoons playing at home, Ophelia and Barb had a routine. Balancing it all, Barb was always rushing from one place to the next. And because of this, Ophelia was often the last one left standing in the carpool pickup at school.

"And here she is, coming around the corner on two wheels!" Ms. Brown, the gym teacher, yelled through the loud speaker. It was humiliating every time, but at least most of the time Ophelia was the only kid left on the curb. Ophelia knew Ms. Brown wanted to go home but instead was left outside to wait for Barb to show up.

Instead of going home, Barb took Ophelia back to the office, where Ophelia completed her homework. If Ophelia finished her homework early, Barb gave her tasks to do around the office like filing or alphabetizing ad books to keep her busy. Ophelia would have minded, but Barb always paid her for her work. Afterward, Barb took her out to the stables, where Ophelia watched her mother perfect her form, jumping on her two thoroughbreds each night. Ophelia saw the happiness horses brought to Barb. But, meanwhile, Ophelia was left bored without her own purpose. Ophelia tried to ride horses, but while she loved animals, it was never something that excited her. It was always something that Barb made her do.

Ophelia soon got into soccer and baseball—two things she enjoyed with her friends. Barb and Ophelia began spending less time together, and they drifted apart with every passing year.

Ophelia dreaded the days she'd have to go shopping with Barb. Barb had an idea of how Ophelia needed to dress, and yet Ophelia never liked what Barb put on her. When she tried to pick out her own things, Barb scolded her loudly in public. Ophelia sulked, hating the way everyone within earshot could hear their conversation.

Ophelia grew fearful of Barb because of this. She was afraid of how Barb would react to things for the sake of embarrassing her. The day finally came when Ophelia begged Mickey to take her shopping instead.

Enough time proved this was a pattern in Ophelia's life. She was always afraid Barb would raise her voice or embarrass her somehow in front of her friends or the general public. Ophelia couldn't help feeling envious of her friends who had a warm relationship with their mothers. She never confided in Barb because she feared her reaction in so many ways. Ophelia's path to her self-discovery was a lonely one. Without Barb there to guide her, Ophelia turned inward to make her own decisions, praying they kept her on the right path to find the one thing she wanted: happiness.

6

SPA HEALING

K ate and Lillian made O drive. It was only two and half hours from Park City to the Mountain Retreat Spa, and O had just turned sixteen, so she was excited to be behind the wheel of Lillian's Suburban. Kate sat in the back with a cup full of chardonnay, flipping through the latest issue of Vogue. Lillian rode shotgun with one of five maps sprawled out in her lap and several books about the great outdoors at her feet.

O was navigating high school and learning what it was like to live with the consequences of her choices. Kate was coming to terms with the fact that her relationship with Peter was over. And Lillian was just trying to escape from her own reality, as usual. She was happiest when she was planning her next adventure. All three women sat in silence, deep in thought, as they drove though the Utah terrain. All three were desperately trying to escape, hoping the trip away would heal them from what they'd left behind.

Kate looked out her window at the rolling hills, but she didn't really see them. She couldn't see the beauty for all the pain inside her. The breakup with Peter was like a physical weight on her chest. Every breath felt like work. It was one of the hardest things she'd ever had to get over. Peter was one of the great loves of her life. Smart, witty, loud, and ambitious, Peter was full of life. Kate thought of how he'd swept her off her feet that first year in San Francisco. He was so unlike the other men she'd allowed in her life. She would never forget the first time she heard his loud laugh at happy hour. He had a zest for life that she found irresistible. So did everyone else around him. And he made her laugh.

For Peter's part, he'd been drawn in by Kate's southern, good-girl nature. He loved her ambition and the fact that she had a mind of her own and a beauty that would take anyone's breath away.

They'd been so happy together in San Francisco. They shared a love of good food and wine and skiing during the winter and spring. Kate felt the ache of their separation. She had let Peter in in a way she never had with any man before. She had always been cautious. But Peter won his way into her heart. He was more than a lover; he'd became her best friend. They were both highly ambitious people determined to take on the world together. Peter had supported her in every move she made and had always been there for her.

He was a lifeline for her. She'd left Texas and her family behind, hoping to start over for good when she made her move to San Francisco on her own.

"Kate only comes to Texas now if there's a funeral,"

Dee was fond of saying. Kate knew Dee was disappointed at how she was distancing herself from the family. But the job in California gave her the kind of financial stability she needed to live her own life in the way she'd always dreamed of. And Peter was the icing on the cake. He embraced her with open arms. He'd even taken the chance to fly to Texas to meet Kate's family. Barb and Dee were happy Kate had finally found someone and couldn't wait to have him spend time with the family. It was the husbands who were the problem.

Ophelia would never forget the first time she met Peter. It was Peter's first trip to Texas ever and the family was determined to give him a warm welcome.

Chuck and Mickey, always up to no good when they were together, felt the need to "initiate" Peter into being married to a Harold woman. Peter had never been to Texas, and Chuck and Mickey felt it was the perfect opportunity to properly welcome him. They dressed up as hicks and roped Trenton and Ophelia into the fun. Dee and Barb picked up Peter from the airport that day, having no idea what their husbands had planned. Knowing Peter was a northerner, Mickey and Chuck took this as opportunity to show him some southern style.

Mickey put in fake crooked teeth and greeted Peter at the front door. Barb and Dee were too stunned to speak. They just shook their heads and let Mickey go on with his joke.

In came Ophelia. "Daddy, what do I do with these chicken guts? The dogs won't eat them!"

Followed by Trenton. "Pa, the goats are loose in the alley again!"

"Where is your Uncle Chuck?" Mickey asked.

"He's getting down to the steel . . . shooing off all those homeless people," Trenton replied.

In walked Chuck holding a bottle of Jack Daniels. "Those damn homeless people just won't get out of here."

Dee and Barb were mortified for their little sister. But Peter just laughed hysterically. All was as it should be, and he was easily taken into the family. Seeing Kate happy made the rest of the family happy. Knowing she had someone brought peace to all, especially living states apart.

The love story of Peter and Kate would end a year later. Kate's world had turned upside down. He announced not only that he was leaving Kate, he was also leaving San Francisco and moving back to New York. He promised her they would always be friends. Kate, brokenhearted, watched a great love of her life walk away.

Ophelia, Lillian, and Kate were all together in Park City the winter after it happened. Kate and O had been skiing all morning at Deer Valley resort, Kate racing fast down the hill just like she always did and O doing everything possible to keep up with her. The girls had stopped for lunch to sample the resort's famous turkey chili. It was always Kate and O's favorite, the perfect warm-up on a cold day on the mountain. Lillian met up with the girls for lunch. Something about slowing down and smelling that comforting bowl of soup made Kate's happiness start slipping. Everyone had gotten their food, made their way to the table, and just sat down when Kate burst into tears.

"Don't cry, Auntie Kate," said O as she set her tray down and reached over to hug her. Ophelia had seen Kate cry many times, but never like this. Kate shook harder but pulled herself together as she looked over at one of the waiters. "You better bring me another beer."

"I hate that man. I really do, Kate. I don't ever want to see him near this family again," said Lillian angrily. Lillian had been holding a grudge against Peter since the moment Kate broke the news of their separation. They had welcomed him into the family, and he'd repaid them by breaking Kate's heart. Lillian never fully accepted the men in her daughter's lives. None were ever good enough, and those who brought pain to them would never be forgiven.

O kept her eyes on the road, deep in thought about the past couple of years. It was a cool summer day that day. She knew she was running away from her life back in Texas; that's what this trip was about for her. There was just something powerful in the mountains of Utah that always put O's soul at peace. She could come here and think about things and put pain behind her. She knew she'd be able to return home feeling brand new in time for the school year.

Ophelia couldn't wait to get past high school. People were always telling her it was the best time of life, but it didn't feel that way to her. High school was just a phase to get her to the life she truly wanted. O had always been one of the most popular girls in school; she had plenty of friends. Her beauty and kind, caring heart always drew people to her. Making friends always came easily to her, and she took care of her friends—she was there for the people she loved.

The best thing about her high school years was meeting her best friend, Amy. Ophelia and Amy had an instant connection. They both had high ambitions for the women they wanted to be; they dreamed of finding their perfect love story. Although they were completely different people, their intellect was what bonded them. Their friendship had grown through their high school years, and they were each other's biggest supporters. It was a friendship Ophelia never took for granted; she knew she was lucky to find someone to walk alongside her and be there for her, no matter what.

Ophelia's natural ability to make friends gave her that tight inner circle. Loyalty and trust were two values she swore to live by. Her beauty and kindness toward others put her in the spotlight, which she'd never really cared for. Ophelia had long, golden-brown hair, bright brown eyes, and a smile that naturally drew people to her. Aside from her friends, she felt lost in the world of high school. Popularity wasn't enough; it had never interested her. Unfortunately, she didn't know what truly interested her. She dreamed of having a successful life, but she was unsure of how to get there.

And then there was her high-school boyfriend. If life taught O anything, it was that she always fell for the bad boy. She found herself drawn to the ones with the most trouble. It was like a compulsion—she could heal them or save them if she showed them true love and compassion. She had so much love to give, but at such a young age she didn't understand the consequences of letting down her guard.

Ophelia took a deep breath and focused on the road in front of her, wishing to blot out thoughts of Jeremy. She just wanted to escape. She hated this feeling of regret. The choice she made was one she could never undo, and it stabbed her like a dagger in the heart. It felt like a gaping wound too large to heal.

She had entered high school a naïve girl with the hopes of finding her sweetheart. She wanted that silly love story that she always dreamed of. Only in hindsight could Ophelia see that she'd been wrapped up in a fantasy with no idea that the choices she'd made were leading her down the wrong path.

"Just be everyone's friend. You don't need to date right now," Barb had told her in the early days of high school. That was one thing her mother had been right about. But how could she have known when her mother had been wrong about so many other things? How could she know who to trust? All Ophelia knew was that she wanted a boyfriend, and her mother's advice didn't align with that. So she'd followed her own ideas about what was right.

Jeremy was the handsome pitcher of the baseball team. He had his eye on Ophelia the moment she walked into the halls of that high school. Everyone warned Ophelia about him, but she couldn't see that his intentions for her weren't pure. He was a ladies' man always getting into trouble. But he had taken her under his wing and made her feel that she was the only girl he had eyes for. It was too late by the time Ophelia learned there were other girls hidden in the shadows. It was young puppy love, and O fell for every bit of it. It was more the *idea* of Jeremy that she fell for, the high-school fantasy of being the popular girl with the popular boy; they were meant to be together.

O remembered how Amy tried to warn her. "He's definitely one of the best-looking guys at school. But do you really want to date him? He's such a player," Amy said to Ophelia one day at lunch. Ophelia knew of his reputation, but she believed she could change him. She really would be the only girl for him.

Of course that hadn't turned out to be true. They went out for over a year, breaking up and getting back together. Jeremy cheated on her with other girls and always begged O to forgive him. He passed Ophelia long notes in between classes, explaining that she was the only one he wanted.

O always forgave him and fell back into the patterns of their relationship. *Why do I do that?* she wondered, watching the trees slip by her in one long blur of green. She could see now that Jeremy had been playing with her. He was out to prove that he could break her down. She was beautiful and smart, independent and capable, and he wanted O eating out of the palm of his hand. The thought of it made her sick. And it hadn't stopped there.

It was Jeremy who had introduced Ophelia to abusing alcohol.

"Just try it, Ophelia . . . we're going to have a fun night. It's you and me, my little peanut," Jeremy told her as she drank that first cold cup of keg beer. She remembered the taste of it . . . that bitter taste one has towards beer when they try it for the first time. It went down so easily, and she actually enjoyed the attention that Jeremy gave her as she fell into a buzzed state. He had a way of influencing her, and she felt like his.

Growing up in a household with women who always drank, it was inevitable that Ophelia would be drawn to drinking, as well. It seemed perfectly normal to get drunk, even at the age she was, because that was what she had grown up around all those years. But then there was the pot and the pills, too—also from Jeremy—that made her forget so many of their nights out together. Jeremy was a part of that life, and Ophelia would find herself joining it, not because she wanted to but because she felt as if she had to to be with him. Ophelia hated the way they made her lose control of herself. Before she knew it, she'd slipped into the high school scene of alcohol and drugs.

Ophelia tried to hold off the memory, but it was rolling toward her like a wave. She'd fallen for Jeremy's biggest trick of all. He'd taken her virginity, and she'd let him. He had been trying to convince her to have sex with him for months. He threatened to leave her and ruin her, in the next breath saying how much he cared about her. She felt he adored her, but as soon as he pressured her, she was drowning in self-doubt. It was a sick manipulation.

Finally one night with the right amount of alcohol, Jeremy had convinced her. Ophelia had one too many shots of vodka and shared a bowl of weed with Jeremy.

"We're going to finally do this tonight, Ophelia. And just think how happy we'll both be," Jeremy had said. "Remember, you're my baby peanut. We'll be together forever."

Jeremy always called her that, peanut. It was the nickname he used with her when he was trying to get what he wanted. Ophelia saw it all play out again in her mind's eye. Her knuckles grew white where they gripped the steering wheel. He was leading her down the hallway and into that dark room. She was on the bed, Jeremy leering above her. It wasn't what Ophelia had imagined, her first time having sex. She didn't enjoy it one bit. She could still see it, the rage and satisfaction in Jeremy's eyes as he conquered her one piece at a time. She was so scared and frightened from the moment it began to the moment it was over.

What had she done? When it was over, she lay there, fearful of what it meant. Her head spun from the cheap vodka, and she finally dozed off.

She woke the next morning alone in a mysterious place and with a headache from all the alcohol. Jeremy was nowhere to be found. He had done it. He had convinced her to do something she never dreamt of doing at that age. She picked up her things and found her way home, so embarrassed and ashamed. She buried herself in her room for days on end.

Once he'd gotten what he always intended from her, Jeremy cast Ophelia aside like garbage. He never cared about her or what would happen to her, which he made clear in the following months. He harassed her in the hallways every time they crossed paths. He spread rumors about her and paraded his conquest of her to the entire school.

Ophelia felt she'd aged overnight, and she vowed to herself that no man would ever take advantage of her or make a mockery of her again. Her heart was broken into a million pieces, not for the man she had lost, but for what he had done to her. He shattered her dream of the perfect romance. She no longer felt hopeful about her future. Jeremy had stolen her comfort and ability to simply be happy in a relationship. She felt even now how cautious she had become. She was suspicious of every boy who looked her way now. Jeremy had broken her and left her ashamed of herself.

She remained focused on the road. Kate still stared off into space. There was nothing but the mountains around her. Her body felt overheated from thinking about all that had happened. She rolled down the window to let the cool mountain breeze in, her arm dangling out the window as she sped down the highway.

How could you have been so blind? Ophelia berated herself.

Not long after the events of that night, Ophelia ran off to Utah, her safe haven away from her world back home. She hadn't been there longer than a week when she got a phone call from Amy. There had been some big high-school party that night, and Jeremy was running his mouth about his conquest over Ophelia. He had "taken the beautiful Ophelia"! Trenton was there and overheard. He was so angry he tackled Jeremy to the ground and threw punch after punch until his friends had to pull him off.

Finding out that Trenton had caught wind of things broke Ophelia's heart even more. She was ashamed to look Trenton in the eye. As her older brother, he had always taught her to be brave and strong and to not take shit from anyone. She knew how disappointed he was in her for letting herself get dragged into this mess. She could tell he was angry with her. She was better than this. He warned her multiple times to walk away. But she didn't listen. She wished she had.

It drove a wedge between Trenton and Ophelia. That was another thing Jeremy had taken from her. She no longer felt comfortable being open with Trenton; she was too afraid of what he thought of her.

"O, you should have seen the look in Trenton's eyes. Had the boys not pulled him off, he probably would have killed him," Amy said to O on the phone that night.

Ophelia said nothing. All she could think was that everyone knew now, including Trenton. How could she face him?

"O! Say something!" yelled Amy.

But she could hardly talk. All she could think was how ashamed she was that everyone knew what had happened that night. She thanked Amy for the phone call and hung up.

Ophelia spent the next three hours sitting on the deck of the home Lillian and Kate had bought together in Utah, staring off into the mountains. Kate joined her a while later. Kate already knew what had happened because Trenton had told Barb, and Barb had of course told the entire family. Barb called Kate screaming and crying, and Kate tried in vain to calm her down. Kate sat down in the chair next to her on the balcony, staring off into the dark sky over the mountains they both loved.

Kate knew Ophelia didn't need a lecture; Barb would have an earful for O when she returned home. That was classic Barb; she'd lecture Ophelia on the ways of the world as she saw them. Ophelia remembered how they'd sat there, side by side in silence, just staring off into space and taking in the crisp mountain air.

That thought filled her with renewed calm for the first time on the drive. This was right. This was the perfect time for both of them to get away. Together they'd work on healing what was broken inside of them. They would do it together.

"Turn here!" screamed Kate.

O snapped out of her daze and barely made the turn in time. She slowed and trundled down the road toward the Mountain Retreat Spa. The front entrance was a white stone building with the red rock setting off magnificent Utah in the background. O pulled the Surburban into the circular drive, trying to slow her racing heart. When they parked and exited the car, they were greeted by a large woman named Susan, dressed in all white and sporting a headband around her forehead.

"Welcome, ladies, to your spa getaway in paradise. I'm Susan. We're so excited to have you here."

"Well, I'm sorry for coming in on two wheels. My granddaughter here just started driving not too long ago, and I can already see she drives just like her damn mother," yelled Lillian, shattering the tenuous peace Susan had just established.

O stepped forward to be greeted by a young twenty-something man wearing a white T-shirt that was clearly two sizes too small for his enormous biceps. He started to unload the car while Susan led the three women to their house, where they'd be staying the week, while rambling on about the history of the spa.

O didn't know what to expect, as Lillian signed the three of them up for that week. For all O knew, Lillian found this place in another one of her travel books. Of course, all Kate and O had needed to hear was "spa" and their bags were packed and ready to go. Kate trained O at a young age to appreciate spa treatments and understand the necessity of facials and massages in a woman's life. They were, after all, the "princesses" in the family. The three ladies linked arms and followed Susan to their retreat. They planned to escape from reality for a solid week.

"Okay, ladies, I hope you like your living quarters. In this book you'll find all the classes we have to offer, as well as the times and schedules for the morning hikes. Breakfast, lunch, and dinner are served at eight, noon, and six. Do not be late! Snacks are available in the main common areas. Here is a list of your daily spa treatments with times and locations. It's important that you arrive ten to fifteen minutes before your treatment begins. Oh, and just one last thing, ladies—we are a completely alcohol-free spa resort, so no beer, wine, or liquor on the premises. Enjoy your stay with us, and if you need anything at all, please don't hesitate to call. Thanks so much!" said Susan as she joyfully exited the casita.

Kate immediately spun around. "What the hell did you sign us up for, Lillian? I can't even have a glass of wine in this joint?"

Lillian shrugged. Ophelia giggled at her aunt. They were in for some serious bonding time.

The next morning, O, Lillian, and Kate woke early in order to catch their hikes. Lillian took the beginners one-hour hike while Kate and O took the more rigorous three-hour hike, which involved some rock climbing and repelling. Kate and O laughed the whole way, taking in the pristine air and the beauty of the Utah mountains. There was something about climbing up the side of a mountain and testing your own strength and endurance that could completely take a person's mind off everything else.

Kate and O fought hard to race each other up the side of the mountain only to repel back down, free as birds. It was on that mountain that both women finally let go of everything bothering them. Though neither truly understood the depth of hurt felt by the other, they knew they needed to heal. They were here for some serious me time. Improving their health through clean eating, exercise, meditation, and of course spa treatments, being cut off from the rest of the world, was a surefire path to healing the cracks of a broken woman.

They left so much of their pain on that mountain that day. Upon their return to the spa's main lobby, they found a small crowd of spa workers surrounding a woman on a chair.

"Oh jeez, it's Lillian," said O to Kate. The two rushed over. There was Lillian, plopped over in a chair, her oversized T-shirt drenched in sweat. Her short red hair was frazzled, and she sported a bright red-and-blue bandanna wrapped around her head. Her eyes were obscured by a pair of oversized sunglasses, and her neck was weighed down by a camera and binoculars. O noticed that the maps were still sticking out of her side pockets.

"I take it the hike didn't go well," Kate said to Lillian.

"Well, I made it about halfway through and just

couldn't go any farther. They said the hike was a beginners hike. HA! More like advanced!" Lillian huffed.

Lillian had been overweight for some time now after years of unhealthy choices and excuses. She'd stepped off the path of health long ago and hadn't managed to get back since; giving up was a common theme in Lillian's life.

"All right. Well, you feel okay now, right? Let's go get some lunch," said Kate. She turned to O. "Aren't you glad we weren't on that hike?"

"What do you mean? We could have hiked alongside Willie Nelson," teased O. Ophelia had found a striking resemblance between her grandmother and the famous singer that day.

Kate laughed. Teasing Lillian was a family tradition, one Lillian had grown used to by now.

O and Kate pulled Lillian up and locked arms with her as they headed into the café for lunch.

The next morning, Lillian decided she'd had it with the hiking and opted for the water aerobics class or, as Kate and O nicknamed them, the "water weenie" class. Kate and O took another morning hike and attended kickboxing and yoga classes. It was the kickboxing that Kate and Ophelia enjoyed most—it was the perfect way to work out all that anger and hurt, beating and kicking the living shit out of the bags assigned to them. They went through the entire sixty minutes without giving up once. Later that afternoon, they both tried to rest their minds in a yoga class, but by that time they couldn't stop laughing at each other. It was something about working their bodies into pretzel shapes while trying to remain calm and quiet that kept cracking them up.

Once Lillian finished in water weenie world, the three women met up for their assigned meals each day. The dishes usually contained vegetables, lettuce, and nuts, with an occasional side of what O could only compare to seaweed. Kate and Ophelia talked about how great a steak would taste right about then to keep their mind off the seaweed they were eating. And, of course, the women had their daily spa treatments, which ended up being their favorite part of the trip.

On the last night of their stay, Ophelia opted for the Epsom salt bath. She was sent to a private room filled with roses and candles, where she lay in the hot bath with light music playing in the background. Once again, as with every other spa session, the music was Enya. Though it was redundant to Ophelia, she enjoyed the peaceful sounds. This was the end of summer and her three-month long trip in the mountains. She had to return to Dallas now and face the reality of the remainder of her high-school years. She dreaded returning, but she knew she had to face the music, the people, and Jeremy. She held her knees tight to her chest and stared at the water around her. She felt so tiny in that room and so alone. What had she done? She was a smart girl. Why had she let it get that far? She was better than all of this, and she knew it. Ophelia made a deal with herself right then to bury the pain deep within her and never look back upon it. She hoped one day she would forget it all.

By the end of the week, all three women were craving a cheeseburger. After checking out, they drove straight to the nearest burger restaurant and inhaled the food within a matter of minutes.

O was scheduled to fly home the next day to prepare for school, which was starting in a couple of days. Just the thought of adjusting back to the real world made O miss Lillian and Kate, though they still sat across from her, wolfing down their burgers. Her summers with them in the mountains were some of the greatest memories of her life. She always felt so free there, away from it all, tucked inside the gorgeous scenery, out of reach of all that could harm her. The three of them were so happy together in those times. Their support reminded her she was loved unconditionally—for who she was, no matter what choices she made.

Ophelia's cell phone buzzed. She fumbled for it but couldn't get it out of her purse in time. By the time she held it in her hand, it was ringing for the third time. It was Amy. She hadn't spoken to her in weeks—since she'd last called to give the Trenton update. O's stomach clenched at the sound of Amy's worried voice. Right there in that burger stand in a tiny Utah town, Ophelia learned that Jeremy had been involved in a horrific car accident. No one knew if he was going to live. As she hung up the phone, O's heart sank and she felt herself slipping into shock.

"What's the matter with you?" asked Kate.

"It's Jeremy," replied O.

"What the hell does that asshole want?"

"He's been in a car accident. He may not make it," O said slowly. "I need to get home."

Neither Kate nor Lillian knew what to say. The happiness Ophelia had achieved over the last week vanished before their eyes. Just like that, O was sucked back into dealing with the saga of the very thing they had hoped to free her from that summer. Kate just pulled Ophelia into her arms and hugged her tightly.

"Do what you have to do. But, remember, you don't owe him anything," Kate said.

It was a long plane ride back to Dallas. Ophelia sat in her seat and stared out the window the entire time. She watched the mountains slowly disappear from sight and the clouds take over. There was so much emotion running through her. The pain Jeremy had caused her was still there inside like a heavy stone, but something in her told her she needed to be at that hospital. Amy was waiting for her at the airport when she landed. Ophelia instructed her to drive straight to the hospital.

"You don't have to do this, O. After everything he has done to you, you don't owe this to him at all."

"I know that, Ames. Please just drive," O said quietly.

She walked calmly into the Parkland Hospital room to find Jeremy lying flat in the bed, completely unable to move. Pins ran up and down the side of his body, holding his broken spine and neck in place. He was strapped down, unable to move anything but his hands and his eyes.

The once strong and arrogant boy Ophelia had known was completely broken into pieces. He had gotten recklessly drunk and flipped his 4Runner several times before it eventually slammed into the median, hitting a large electrical pole. He had managed to pull himself out of the car, holding his neck in place. Bystanders called 911, and Jeremy was rushed to the emergency room. Doctors said it was a miracle he survived, but he would never be the same. His broken neck and spine indicated he would most likely be paralyzed.

His hospital room was packed full of friends from school. Everyone looked at Ophelia as she walked in. She was a ghost to them, having vanished during the last couple of months. She could tell from their faces they were shocked that she had even shown up.

O stood at the end of the bed, staring at Jeremy, at the person who had broken her into so many pieces just eight months ago. He looked shaken and scared. This was definitely not the boy she remembered.

"Hey, everybody, thanks for coming," Jeremy said. He was barely able to talk. "But can everyone please clear out and give me a moment alone with O?"

As the group shuffled out of the room, Jeremy motioned with his eyes for O to close the door and come closer. O moved toward the side of his bed. He reached for her hand, though the restraints didn't let his hand get far. Ophelia stood silent and motionless, looking down at his hand trying to reach for her. She stared him up and down, seeing that his body was completely pinned together, holding him in place.

"Thanks for coming, O," he said. "I don't know why you came, and I don't deserve your presence here, but I'm glad you came to be here for me." Ophelia continued to stare at him as she sat down in the chair next to his bed.

She couldn't stand any longer, and she still couldn't speak. This boy had destroyed her just a short time ago, and here he was in the aftermath of a horrific accident that nearly took his life.

Tears welled up in his eyes and rolled down his cheeks.

"I'm so sorry, Ophelia. For everything . . . everything I ever did to you. I'm sorry. I'm an asshole for putting a perfectly innocent girl through that. You didn't deserve how I treated you. I don't know why you're here. I don't deserve you being here for me. But I'm glad you are. It just shows who you are, and I'll always admire that about you."

O stared back at him. She believed him and received his apology. It seemed unfair that it took a horrific accident for Jeremy to see the light, but she was ready to move on.

"I forgive you," Ophelia said, reaching over and gently squeezing his hand. "Now rest and get better, please." She leaned down to kiss his forehead and then she left the room.

She left the hospital with Amy, returning often to visit Jeremy until he'd healed. He eventually did learn to walk again. She forgave him. That powerful thing about forgiveness, Ophelia thought, was that you could accept a person's actions from the past and move on with the present. She understood that forgiveness was something necessary to picking herself up and moving on. Living with a grudge or hate was not something O was built to handle. Jeremy would never be allowed to disrespect her ever again.

. . .

Months later, he left the hospital and returned to school. Though he and Ophelia never got back together or rekindled the relationship they once had, they remained friends for the rest of their high school years. Ophelia didn't ask for his friendship, but she let him be her friend in whatever capacity he wanted. Still, she never forgot what he'd done. She lived with that for the rest of her life. The consequences stayed with her too.

From that time on, Ophelia would forever be a cautious woman.

7

THE LAST CHRISTMAS

I t was the last Christmas the Harolds ever spent together as a family. Everyone gathered at the condo Lillian and Kate had purchased together in Utah. The whole family, as Ophelia had known it as a child, would have one last Christmas together before things changed forever.

It was a miracle that Chuck and Dee made the trek out to Utah. Dee hardly traveled anywhere by this time, unless it was for work. But this was to be her last holiday in the United States before her company would transfer her to South America for the next several years.

Lillian was just happy to have all three of her daughters and her two grandchildren under the same roof for Christmas. She had been lonely the last couple of months all by herself at the Harold home. She'd spent her days ordering junk from infomercials and watching the mail pile up. She never threw away a piece of mail because she told herself she would eventually get through it all. Lillian had quit her job teaching at the local university, preferring to teach online courses. She woke up every morning watching Fox News, spent her time grading a few papers, then watched old movies she'd seen too many times to count. It kept her busy most days, and it was the routine she counted on to get through each day.

Since Kate had left for San Francisco, it was rare to see her at family gatherings back in Texas, so the family Christmas had to come to her this year. Kate was proud of her independence and self-made success. She had worked hard to provide herself with the life she always wanted. Lillian was just happy that Kate had picked herself up and built her own life. She'd watched her youngest daughter hoping and dreaming for too many years. Finally, Kate had taken action and was now reaping the rewards. The only downside now was that Lillian worried about her daughter being out in California all alone.

Kate was proud of her success. And she was proud of the second home that she and Lillian had purchased together. Park City was her escape from reality, something she shared with her niece. She spent increasingly more time out there, packing up her Pathfinder with her two Labradors on Thursdays to make the eleven-hour drive to Park City for a long weekend.

This was the first time she'd had the entire family up to Park City for a holiday. She couldn't help wondering if it would be the only time. It felt like life was changing too fast for everyone to keep up.

Trenton, who had been in college for a year now, had managed to make the trip over his winter break. He wouldn't admit it to anyone at the gathering, but he was worried about his parents. He'd watched Mickey and Barb's marriage slowly falling apart for years. Trenton, the eternal optimist, always thought things would stay the same no matter what, but even he couldn't see a way forward for his parents.

The couple's rocky relationship was no secret to Ophelia either. She saw how beaten down and tired Mickey was and couldn't help thinking a divorce was inevitable any day now. Watching Mickey and Barb was like watching two strangers. Ophelia sensed the end was coming soon. There was only so much a person could endure before it was time to pick up and move on.

Despite the impending changes coming for their family, Ophelia tried to put it aside for this trip. Whatever was meant to happen one day between Mickey and Barb would happen. Ophelia wouldn't be in the house much longer; soon she'd be an adult living on her own. For this Christmas, she was just glad to be in her happy place, and she was excited to hit the slopes every day with Trenton and Kate. Her own issues were starting to boil deep down, but for this winter break, she chose to bury her worries and put her energy toward enjoying the time off. She was determined to escape to her happy place and the peace that the mountains brought to her soul.

Christmas Eve morning, Ophelia woke to the winter wonderland she had always dreamed of. She had slept snuggled up next to Kate. For as long as she could remember, she slept next to Kate when they were together. Kate was the big sister and friend she never had. Kate understood Ophelia, most likely because they shared a lot of the same emotions and reactions toward things. Kate was the successful career woman Ophelia hoped to become one day. Kate also had an inner child and need for excitement that Ophelia hoped she would never lose as she got older. Ophelia saw a strong woman in Kate. She was a woman who navigated through this world without the help of anyone around her. The feeling was mutual; Kate saw much of herself in Ophelia and had taken her under her wing from early on.

Ophelia was eager to get out on the slopes for a few runs before the big dinner that night. Kate was still asleep beside her, snuggled up in the sheets and blankets, dreaming away as Ophelia looked out the window at powdered snow covering the mountain behind the house. The beauty of it took O's breath away every time she woke to that sight. The scenery of the large, rugged mountains always made Ophelia feel so small; she was living in a world so much bigger than her. It made every issue she was feeling inside seem small and irrelevant. It also made her dream big and feel powerful to take control of her life. The mountains always gave O the fuel she needed to return back to her life.

Ophelia hugged her knees to her chest and smiled, staring down at Kate, who slept so peacefully. Ophelia didn't want to wake her just yet. Instead, she ran down two flights of stairs to find Mickey, Chuck, and Lillian in the kitchen. Lillian and Chuck sat at the breakfast table, completely zoned into Fox News, making political, right-wing comments here and there. Mickey was at the stove firing up omelets for the entire family; the glazed look in his eyes told Ophelia he was off in his own world.

"Is Trenton up?" Barb asked, coming down the stairs and fumbling with her robe. "And where the fuck is the coffee?" Mickey just stared at her and pointed to the brewing coffee pot.

Ophelia took notice of the cold distance between Mickey and Barb. The two never had a history of showing much outward affection, but something had distinctly changed between them in the last several years. It was almost as if they had stopped paying attention to one another.

Next down the stairs was Dee with a cigarette hanging out of her mouth, blowing smoke into the kitchen. She had packed a day bag full of cigarettes and any other pertinent supplies she'd need for the day. She planned to sit in the kitchen all day and avoid going upstairs again unless she had to.

"Dee, not inside. Go!" Lillian said, motioning toward the balcony.

"It's twenty fucking degrees outside. Blow me," replied Dee. But she grabbed Barb's mink coat hanging on one of the chairs by the balcony door and went outside to finish her cigarette. "A poor animal had to die so Barb could have her coat," Dee said sarcastically as she walked toward the door.

"Whatever, Dee. That is the warmest coat you will ever wear. Your skinny ass will be glad you have it on in about ten minutes," Barb yelled back at her. The joking never stopped between Dee and Barb, but the love and friendship between them remained.

Last down the stairs was Trenton, followed by a sleepy Kate. Trenton and Kate were always last to wake up. They were never in a hurry to get anywhere. They lived life as it came to them.

The family sat around the giant oak table that Lillian and Kate had purchased for the condo's dining room. Lillian and Kate had spent the last year furnishing the home to make it their perfect mountain escape. They were proud to be able to share it with the family. Trenton, Kate, and Chuck inhaled most of their food, as usual. Barb fussed over Ophelia's messy hair. Ophelia drifted off into another world, ignoring her mother. Lillian told Barb to leave Ophelia alone. Dee barely ate, as was her habit. Ophelia always figured she smoked so many cigarettes she probably couldn't taste anything. Mickey sat silently reading the newspaper.

Mickey drove everyone out to the mountains later in the day—except for Dee and Chuck, who would remained at the house, probably drinking, smoking, and watching television all day. Lillian, Barb, and Kate fussed in the car the whole time. Kate and Barb took cheap shots at each other any chance they got. Lillian told them to hush and complained about another health reason preventing her from skiing like the rest of them. Trenton intervened, trying to find some peace between them. Mickey and Ophelia rode up front, content to sit in silence together.

Once they arrived at the mountain resort and everyone unloaded, Mickey and Ophelia were the last ones out of the car. Mickey looked at O and joked, "Get me away from these women!" Ophelia laughed at her dad, but she also knew on some level he was being serious.

On ski days, Lillian and Barb skied together on the lower mountain because of the easier trails. Barb looked out for Lillian; she would not leave her mother alone on a mountainside. Barb had grown increasingly protective of Lillian over the years. Barb had suffered her fair share of injuries, making her cautious. Ophelia always thought of Barb like a china doll. When she wasn't too careful, she broke easily. Barb had broken her back and fractured her neck, and she had terrible knees. Lillian suffered from a heart condition and osteoporosis. Lillian always told O it was because of bad bones, but Ophelia suspected it was just from her grandmother's poor health decisions. Lillian and Barb may as well have been on the permanent injury list for every ski trip the family took together. But they got their few runs in on the bunny trail and then called it a day.

Mickey skied solo, usually on the trails winding around the mountains through the ski-in, ski-out homes. Mickey had never been a big skier and basically learned after being married to Barb. He much preferred a leisurely golf game. Kate always joked, "Mickey likes to get in his two to three runs and look at all the beautiful houses and then go sit at the lodge and drink Coors Light until we all get done."

On the upper side of the mountain, Ophelia was flying down the slope, determined to beat Kate and Trenton. Kate was a fast skier and had become an expert during her more frequent trips out to Park City. Trenton and Ophelia usually only made it out to Park City once in the winter, but they did everything they could to keep up with Kate. Ophelia thought of when she'd first learned to ski. Lillian put her in ski school at eight years old. On the fourth day, after three days of ski school, Kate took her out for her first real adventure on the mountain.

"All right, now that you have the basics down, no more of that bunny slope shit. I'm really going to teach you how to ski," Kate had told her. She remembered Kate sitting beside her on the lift as it whisked them straight up to the top of the mountain.

"Remember the basics of how to navigate your skis. The rest is all mental. Now don't be a wuss, and figure out your way down this hill. I don't like to wait on slow skiers, so don't forget to keep up with me." Ophelia just nodded at Kate, pointed her skis downhill, and followed her aunt all the way down the mountain. She didn't want to be left behind. Though she relished the feel of the wind on her face and the thrill of winning, she admitted to herself that Kate's words all those years ago had never left her. She didn't want to make Kate wait on her; she was always working to keep up.

Later that night, the whole family gathered for dinner. As usual, a large meal had been prepared, and the alcohol was flowing. Dee had a head start on everyone because she had spent most of the day guzzling her chardonnay while everyone else was on the mountain. It didn't take long, though, for Barb and Kate to catch up to their older sister.

The argument between Barb and Kate started out like every argument between them. It was a series of small, low blows, one after another, the sisters taking stabs at each other. The small, subtle comments started at the dinner table. Barb couldn't help making a snide remark about Kate's new life out in San Francisco and her most recent failed relationship. Kate responded with a blow at Barb for always playing the victim in everything and never taking ownership of her actions.

Dee came to Barb's defense, as she always did. Kate got mad about Dee smoking in the house, and Dee got mad at Kate for making her go outside. Lillian intervened, trying to get all her daughters to calm down. But Lillian knew better than to try to control her girls. After all, she'd raised them to stand up for themselves. Too bad raising three alpha females hadn't included lessons in conflict resolution.

By this time, the resentment between Barb and Kate went so deep that there was no hope in sight for the two to ever truly get along. Lillian always assumed they'd grow out of it one day, but there didn't seem to be any hope of that by now.

Trenton sensed the tension growing at the dinner table and saw the ever-growing number of wine bottles piling up. Mickey also sensed the impending fight and motioned for Trenton to take Ophelia out of the room.

The pair went upstairs and out on the deck, where Lillian had a hot tub installed earlier that summer. They sat in the hot tub, catching up and drinking a bottle of Jack Daniels Trenton had smuggled from the kitchen, completely oblivious to what was going on downstairs. Since he'd been away at college, Trenton had been drinking more, which was typical for a Texas frat boy.

Downstairs, the fighting escalated to the point that neither Dee, Barb, nor Kate were making much sense. The three were mostly mumbling. Mickey and Chuck could only look on helplessly as the three sisters tore each other apart. They just shook their heads in disbelief. Mickey was mortified at Barb's behavior; he couldn't stand watching her act this way. For years he'd told his wife to take the high road and just let things go. But Barb had a bigger chip on her shoulder and was raised to speak her mind. She wasn't about to take her husband's advice. Mickey lost his only brother years ago. The two had never been very close, and he regretted every day that they didn't have a better relationship, so it pained him to see Barb sabotaging her connection with her younger sister.

No one was certain who made the first move—it all happened so fast. But within seconds, Barb and Kate were both swinging at each other in a drunken rage. That was the last straw for Mickey and Chuck; they'd had enough. The men had to physically separate Barb and Kate. Chuck grabbed Kate, and Mickey grabbed Barb to pull them apart. Neither was sober enough to be making sense. Dee and Lillian were off to the side watching the drama unfold.

"Barb, that's enough! Look at the two of you. This is Christmas, and you two are tearing each other apart. Thank God Trenton and Ophelia didn't see this," yelled Mickey. He couldn't believe that two middle-aged women couldn't even get through a meal together. But even now Barb refused to listen. She grabbed Dee, and the two retired to the balcony to smoke cigarettes and allow Barb to lick her wounds. Chuck just shook his head at Kate as he released his sister-in-law. "Well, I've had about all I can handle for one night. I'm going upstairs. Merry Christmas." Chuck said as he left the kitchen.

Kate went upstairs to her bed. Mickey helped Lillian

cleaned up the kitchen as she tried to explain the nature of the women to her son-in-law. "We're complicated women, Mickey. Barb doesn't mean the things she says sometimes." Mickey worked silently beside her and tuned her out. He'd had it, and Lillian knew it. She'd always admired and loved Mickey. He had taken care of the family well, but she knew the love story between Mickey and Barb was long over.

For the first time, the family skipped opening presents on Christmas Eve. They unwrapped the packages in the morning, but it was all done without a word, in complete and uncomfortable silence. The women refused to speak to one another, still angry and hungover from the night before. Chuck and Dee flew home later that day, followed by Mickey and Barb. Only Trenton and Ophelia remained behind for a few extra days to ski with Kate and spend more time with Lillian.

Ophelia and Trenton quickly forgot about the Christmas festivities. Watching their mother bicker and fight with their aunts wasn't new to them. They'd become immune to it by this point in their lives. Ophelia always laughed when people joked about their families not being normal. "No, you don't understand—my family is far from normal," Ophelia would say.

It was there at the cabin that Trenton and Ophelia had their first real conversation about that state of their parents' marriage. And once they'd broached the subject, it was like a kind of permission to revisit the topic, which they did frequently through the coming years.

At the tail end of their trip, the four of them sat in the kitchen one night talking everything out and drinking several bottles of wine. Ophelia got the drunkest she'd ever been. Trenton was the one to bring up the subject of his parents. "Okay, so I'm away right now at college, but things between Mom and Dad just seem to be getting worse. Ophelia, what's going on?"

Ophelia didn't really know what to say. She could only talk about how they were rarely ever at the house together. Mickey was traveling constantly, and Barb was away at horse shows. Ophelia spent a great deal of time at the house alone. And when they were together, they hardly said a word to each other.

"Well, I don't know anyone who could live with Barb," Kate said, still reeling from their fight. "Barb scored a good one when she met Mickey, and she's spent most of her life driving him away. Men like Mickey can only take so much before it's time to pick up and move on in search of a better life."

"Now, now . . . Barb is a very sensitive woman. But she's a good woman, and she'll do anything to keep her family together," said Lillian. Lillian was always quick to come to Barb's defense. Kate knew it was true, though; Barb was a sensitive woman. And she would do anything for her family. The problem was that she didn't always see the consequences of her actions, how things she said affected other people. Barb was a good, hard-working, self-made woman. She just didn't always have her emotions in check. And she rarely took ownership of how she reacted to things.

The four of them talked for hours that night until Ophelia lost track of how many times she'd refilled her wine glass. She was seventeen, and she didn't know her limits. She enjoyed the taste of the wine, and she was so locked into the conversations she didn't register the alcohol until it was too late. It hit her all of a sudden as she tried to walk up the stairs to her bedroom. She got short of breath, and her head felt extremely heavy. The nausea rolled over her like a wave, and all she could do was yell for Kate.

She spent the next three hours hurling up every drop of alcohol she had consumed that night. Trenton and Kate sat by her side in the bathroom, laughing at Ophelia for having her first real experience of alcohol poisoning.

"Oh, it happens to the best of us," Kate said, chuckling as she gathered Ophelia's thick, long golden hair and pulled in back into a ponytail.

"Welcome to boozing," Trenton echoed.

They fetched her water and cold towels all night. Ophelia hurled until she was so physically exhausted that she passed out, ignoring the jokes that Trenton and Kate made as they nursed her back to health. When she finally collapsed on the bathroom floor, Trenton carried his sister to bed and tucked her in.

Kate brushed her teeth, put on her pajamas, and crawled in bed next to Ophelia. She didn't want her niece to wake up alone.

The next morning, Ophelia woke to Lillian handing her a tray of Advil, water, orange juice, and breakfast. "You need to eat, honey. You've got nothing in you," she said.

Kate cracked an eye and looked at her mother.

"And, Kate, she's only seventeen. You should have cut her off."

"If she's going to be in this family, she needs to learn

her limits. The girl needs to learn to handle her booze," Kate said giggling.

Lillian rolled her eyes and motioned for Ophelia to sit up and eat.

But Ophelia couldn't move. Her head felt like it weighed a thousand pounds. For the first time she felt the sadness after a night of drinking. The shame spiral it would put her in after a hard night. A shame spiral that she would fall into after every hard night she'd have to come. *So this is the consequence of 'overdoing it,'* she told herself.

Kate and Trenton went skiing a few hours later, leaving Ophelia behind. Lillian lay in bed beside her all day and watched movies with her granddaughter as she recovered from the night before.

Ophelia didn't say much. She mostly stared out the window off into the mountains and found comfort in a dream world.

8

"I'M LEAVING YOUR MOTHER"

By the summer before her senior year in high school, Ophelia was plotting her escape. She would finish her senior year and move far, far away for college. She longed to move out and start a life of her own. Would she move to Virginia? Colorado? Or even London? She looked to go anywhere that took her away from Texas and the life she knew. She was seventeen, but she felt like she was twenty-one. She dreamed of having her own independence. It wasn't that she didn't love the people in her life; she just longed for the distance and to set out on her own path.

She was at a turning point emotionally, and she couldn't keep up with the pain growing inside her. She didn't know what she wanted to be, but she knew who she wanted to be. Ophelia was going to be successful, and she was going to do it without the help of a man.

But first, she planned to spend her senior year with all her friends and have the best possible time. The hurt she buried inside her crept up now and again, but Ophelia had a knack for hiding it well. On the outside, she was the beautiful, popular girl surrounded by friends; but deep down she was fighting anger, pain, and a loneliness she carried with her wherever she went.

Like many of her peers, she dabbled in drinking and doing drugs on the weekend. She smoked weed with her friends and took a few pills here and there. She experimented because everyone else was doing it, and she liked how losing control let her drift off into another world. It was alcohol she turned to the most to take her into the land of forgetfulness. But it was also her biggest enemy.

Ophelia watched for years as Lillian, Barb, Dee, and Kate drowned their tears in alcohol. So it was natural for her to turn to it to escape. Losing control was her escape from her thoughts.

O's senior year brought big changes into her life and Barb's life. The week before school started, O went to her first high-school party as a senior. Barb was gone for the weekend, competing in one of her horse shows. Ophelia was getting ready in her room when her friends honked and hollered for her to come outside and jump in the car. She knew Mickey would be yelling for her any minute.

"Ophelia, can you come in the kitchen for a minute?" hollered Mickey.

It had been just the two of them that weekend. Mickey was as distant as ever, but Ophelia was so wrapped up in her own issues she didn't really take notice. She had actually grown used to both Barb and Mickey being gone. Trenton was away at school, so most of the time Ophelia had the house to herself. She never minded being left alone; she actually enjoyed it. She had friends over whenever she wanted, and when they weren't, Ophelia had time alone with her thoughts.

O came running in to find Mickey sitting on the bar stool at the end of their kitchen bar. He looked beaten down and exhausted. One look at him told Ophelia something serious was going on. She could tell Mickey was having trouble gathering his thoughts. That was the thing about Mickey—he was a great businessman who could talk to anyone and give a speech to a room of hundreds of people, but when it came time to talk about emotions, he sometimes had trouble getting it all out. This always bothered Barb, who wore her heart on her sleeve. That deep emotional connection she longed for had never materialized in her marriage to Mickey.

"I'm on my way out. The girls are honking for me to come out." Ophelia talked quickly, eager to get to the party.

Mickey looked at her long and hard. Seeing the seriousness in his eyes, Ophelia took the seat next to him.

"O, we need to talk. It's been a very long and difficult past couple of years."

Ophelia just stared at her father; she knew what was coming next.

"I've made the decision—I'm leaving your mother," Mickey said. He went on to explain how he was renting an apartment not far down the road and that he'd be close by. He also said he'd be moved out before the weekend was over.

O looked at him, not entirely surprised by the news, but a little in shock at the timing of the message. Not that there was really ever a good time to tell your kids that your parents were breaking up for good. And she'd seen a cold distance between Barb and Mickey for as long as she could remember. The love stories she'd grown up with, and the love story she'd dreamed of for herself, were a far cry from the reality of Barb and Mickey's marriage. She supposed they had loved each other once long ago, but over the years they had become business partners running a household and raising two children. Maybe that was why Barb always ran off to the horse stables, Mickey was gone on business, and O and Trenton were left at home alone.

O saw in Mickey's face that he was finally setting himself free to go and live his own life. She had always adored her father and wanted nothing but his happiness. He had taken care of her, protected her, and always pushed her to be her better self.

Ophelia reached for Mickey's hand and gave it a squeeze. "Go find her, Daddy. Find the love of your life, and find your happiness." She meant it. She wanted true love for both her parents, especially since they didn't have it in one another. They didn't deserve to live their lives this way, pretending to be in a happy, fulfilling relationship. They both deserved people who loved them and fulfilled the life they dreamed of for themselves.

Father and daughter shared a big hug. The SUV waiting for Ophelia honked again, and Ophelia heard the shrill laughter of her friends. O grabbed her bag and keys and headed out the front door.

Trenton would later tell Ophelia about all the arguments he had overheard over the years between Mickey and Barb. "You just don't know everything, Ophelia. There is so much I heard between the two of them. And I'm glad you never heard. Dad wanted out a long time ago, but Mom fought to keep the family together for a long time," Trenton would tell Ophelia over brunch one day years down the road.

Ophelia didn't hold back that night. She partied hard and drank herself into the next day. She cried to Amy, who just held her. Ophelia understood and supported the divorce; she was never angry at them. If anything, she thought this was the best possible thing that could happen to them. She didn't know why she was crying that night— it was the only time she ever got upset about the divorce. Maybe it was because endings were always difficult.

For the next ten months, Barb and Ophelia shared a house together, just the two of them. Those months put permanent damage between Barb and Ophelia, damage they wouldn't recover from for years.

Barb unraveled as she came to terms with the reality of her new normal. She and Mickey attended therapy sessions together, but ultimately they decided divorce was inevitable. Barb fought for the marriage; Mickey had thrown in the towel long ago. He was done. Barb's drinking got worse as she turned to vodka martinis or chardonnay to calm her nerves. Although deep down she knew divorce was right, she had a hard time imagining a different way of life. She spent even more time at the horse stables to cope. It was the only place she felt free, riding in the fields on the back of her thoroughbreds.

Ophelia grew to despise her mother's temper and the emotional rants she unleashed when she had too much to drink. O was changing, too; her adult years were coming on fast, and she already had so much experience behind her. And yet, without a clear path forward, she felt confused and terrified of making the wrong decision. She knew where she ultimately wanted to be, but she was unsure how to get there.

Barb knew Ophelia was slipping farther away from her, and she spent many sleepless nights trying to figure out how to connect with her daughter again. Whatever tenuous bond they'd once shared was gone. Barb chalked it up to teenage angst, justifying her actions by telling herself Ophelia just needed discipline. But that was not what Ophelia needed; she only ever wanted a friend to listen and understand her.

O partied increasingly more during her senior year. She buried the growing ache inside her with marijuana and alcohol. Her focus was set on the next party instead of chasing her dream of leaving it all behind. And Barb's increasing fragility and constant spouts of anger only drove O farther away.

Instead of finding one another in the grief of their dissolving family, mother and daughter drifted farther apart. The difference between them was how they handled their sadness. Barb wore it outwardly like a badge, so openly that Ophelia wondered if Barb was begging for attention. Unlike her mother, Ophelia buried her grief deep down, never wanting to confront it. She saw sadness and pain as weakness and was determined to rise above it.

On New Year's Eve that year, fate stepped into O's life.

Ophelia was looking forward to going out in downtown Dallas with her friends to see a Keller Williams concert. New Year's always marked a new beginning of hope for Ophelia. She took the time to reflect and set intentions for herself, wishing for prosperous change and good fortune ahead for her. No matter how dark things got, she always held out hope that things would get better.

On this New Year's Eve, Ophelia met *him*, the first boy she ever loved. He became the gift she'd always hoped for. Ophelia was sitting on a stool surrounded by friends when he walked right up to her and leaned so far over her that he almost pushed her out of the way. He smiled long and hard at her as if she were the only girl in the room.

"Um, excuse me. I'm sorry, am I in your way or something?" said a blushing Ophelia. He had a smile so big it filled her stomach with butterflies. It was that feeling that she had always heard about but never fully experienced. He was good looking and charming, just as Ophelia had dreamed about. And his eyes were only set on her.

"I'm Travis. I'm the guy who's going to make you laugh and smile. I'm going to take all your troubles away. I've been staring at you all night. I had to be next to you. You're going to come and dance to this song with me," he said.

He grabbed O by the hand and led her into the crowd, where Keller Williams continued to play. By midnight, O was lost in a daze. She danced the night away with Travis, and at midnight he leaned down and kissed her. Ophelia felt the entire world come to a stop.

They joined the crowd running out to dance in the streets behind the band. Ophelia looked up to see a sky full of stars. Looking back at Travis, she grinned, loving the protective way he had about him. It made her feel safe. She felt foolish dancing there with him under the stars on the streets of downtown, feeling like she was already in love. Travis took her under his wing like the protective guy she'd always hoped for. They spent the entire night together until the sun rose the next day to start the new year. He was the fresh start she had been looking for. Everyone she had met before became a distant memory. O saw for the first time what it was like to have a boy adore her and have eyes only for her.

Travis was a college student, and he had to go back to school soon for the new semester. But he made frequent visits to see Ophelia throughout the end of her senior year. He was only two hours away, which made it an easy trip. Travis spent every spare moment he had with her. Ophelia was floating on cloud nine, swept away by his kindness and care. Travis called Ophelia his, and he didn't want anyone else to have her.

He made romantic gestures like showing up unexpectedly at her house with bundles of tulips, O's favorite flowers. With Barb gone most of the time, they had the house to themselves, and it became all about them. Ophelia felt shrouded in a world of their own making, and being with an older guy made her feel grown up too. It didn't matter what was going on in the world around them; all that mattered was Travis looking down into her eyes and kissing her. She'd never been around a boy she couldn't stop kissing. She adored every bit of him. At night, they danced in the living room together to Robert Earl Keen, their favorite Texas country singer. Every song took on special meaning to them. When Travis drove in from college to surprise her, he would say, "I'm Coming Home to You." That Robert Earl Keen song would forever remind Ophelia of Travis. Ophelia was happiest when she was with him; she was able to forget about going off to college soon, about her parent's divorce, and about her deteriorating relationship with her mother.

Barb and Ophelia's relationship continued its downward spiral. Barb was also dating again. She found some temporary happiness in a truck driver named Arnie. Arnie gave Ophelia the creeps, mainly because he seemed to love to drink just as much as Barb did. Ophelia thought Arnie only saw her mother as a wealthy divorced woman who was emotionally unstable, a perfect situation for a man like him to swoop in. Ophelia felt he only enabled her mother's bad habits. She despised him every time he walked into their family's home. And she blamed Barb for bringing the creep into their lives.

Trenton had come home from school one night to stay the weekend with Barb and Ophelia. Arnie got drunk and was passed out on the couch. Trenton and Ophelia took it as an opportunity to draw all over him. He was a joke to her kids, and it took Barb a long time to realize that.

Barb and Ophelia were arguing more than ever. Sometimes it got so bad that O would run off to Mickey's house. O never understood why Mickey hadn't taken her with him. She could only guess that Barb fought to keep her home to try to mend the relationship before O moved out for good. Things were getting worse, and it was piling onto Ophelia like bricks inside of her. She was at her breaking point, and she started to lose it. The depression that had been building climaxed, and she found herself in the biggest fight of her life.

The only time things were normal between Ophelia and Barb was when Travis was around. Barb and Travis liked each other, which helped distract Ophelia from the rift growing between her and her mother. Barb welcomed Travis over whenever he wanted; she could see Ophelia was happiest when he was around, and she loved him for that. And Travis made Barb seem more normal, which brought peace to Ophelia. Travis would often join Barb and Ophelia for dinner and would mix martinis with Barb in the kitchen, laughing alongside her.

O was in love with Travis, but she couldn't defeat the growing emptiness and depression that continued to build inside her. Even Travis's love for her wasn't strong enough to overcome her darkness. It was a battle inside Ophelia only she could defeat; she just didn't know how. Her sadness grew in her like a disease, and no matter how happy Travis made her when she was with him, she couldn't defeat her inner demons and the racing thoughts growing day by day.

Ophelia took out her sadness and anger on Travis, a regret she lived with for the rest of her life. Though he never gave her reason not to trust him, she projected her inner world onto him and refused to put her faith in him. She had only known pain before him, and she expected him to destroy her one day, no matter how happy he made her. Though the wound Jeremy had inflicted healed, she walked with a large scar on her heart.

One night after Ophelia had way too much drink at a party, she called Travis upset and questioning his intentions with her. It wasn't the first time, and it was a stupid move that was getting old. Her residual anger with her humiliation from Jeremy always came up when she'd had too much drink. The loss of control would bring up negative emotions. It was unfair to Travis, and in the beginning he did all he could to bring Ophelia back to her senses.

This time Travis was angry with her. He drove all the way from college that night to come pick Ophelia up off the floor from her friend's party and drive her home. He couldn't believe the state she'd put herself in. Ophelia just sobbed the entire way home. When he pulled into her driveway, they sat there, having the biggest fight of their relationship. O said many things she didn't mean, and Travis argued back at how ridiculous she was being. As they fought, they heard loud Russian music suddenly coming from the backyard and a woman's drunken singing. Ophelia and Travis looked at each other, recognizing the voice was Barb's. The tension dissolved, and they were both laughing hysterically.

"Let's stop fighting. Come on, let's go see what that crazy mother of yours is up to," said Travis, grabbing O's hand and leading her inside.

Travis and O walked in to find Barb sitting on the patio in the backyard with a vodka martini in hand, eyes shut and humming along to Russian symphony. Barb was in another one of her emotional fits, turning to her martini to take away the pain of the divorce.

Naturally, O was embarrassed to find Barb a complete mess. Travis just laughed; he always found Barb's antics to be hilarious. He grabbed her by the hands and danced with her on the patio, and all was as it should be in Travis's arms underneath the stars. Next they put on Robert Earl Keen and listened to "Feelin' Good Again." Travis was happy to see her smile return when he held her in his arms. Barb, O, and Travis stayed up till the early hours of the next morning. It was one of the few good nights Barb and Ophelia shared together. Travis always brought out the best in Barb and Ophelia's relationship, and Ophelia loved him for that. Had it not been for Travis, things would have been worse that year.

Travis stayed over that night, holding Ophelia all night long. He didn't let go of her for a minute. He knew something was wrong, but he couldn't figure it out. Ophelia stayed silent as usual, tucking the pain as far down as she could. Although Travis knew Ophelia wouldn't admit the pain of seeing her family change, he was there for her as much as he could be.

Ophelia didn't understand at the time that it was too much to put on a young guy trying to navigate his own life. That night, Ophelia slept the best she'd slept in a long time. The safety in his arms brought her such a feeling of peace. In the morning, Travis said, "Sweetheart, I have to go back to school now. You be good, okay, kiddo?" Then he kissed her goodbye.

O's heart broke every time she watched him walk away. She was never sure if it would be the last time she saw him. Her residual feelings from her experience with Jeremy were to blame. She felt that every guy who entered her life would leave her, no matter how much he loved her. Ophelia couldn't keep up with what was happening to her, and she was too young to process what it all meant.

As a result, she pushed away the first guy she ever truly loved. It ended just as quickly as it began. Travis and Ophelia had one last night together out with their friends. O had too much to drink and started to drift away in her thoughts. She was lost in her future: where she'd be, how she couldn't wait to get away from Barb, how she wanted to escape everything around her. Her fears that Travis would leave her or would not want the same things as she did took over.

She picked a fight with Travis, and they argued. Standing by his truck outside their friend's house, tears streaming down her face, Ophelia said, "I just can't do this anymore." She didn't mean it, but she felt that if she pushed Travis away, he couldn't leave her because she'd be leaving him first.

Travis got in his truck, slammed the door, and drove off. She watched him leave for the very last time. O got home that night to a text message from Travis: "I hope you know what you're doing. This will be the end of us." And he was right; it was.

Ophelia fell apart after that. Just as being with Travis was the happiest Ophelia had been, things ending between them thrust her into the saddest time of her life. Ophelia did everything in her power to get Travis back. But Travis refused to take O back, no matter how hard she tried. She had taken every ounce of her anger and sadness out on him. He didn't deserve that. She never loved him the way he deserved to be loved. She had been selfish, making everything about her and her struggles without taking the time to properly love him back.

Ophelia eventually realized she couldn't blame him for leaving her. He deserved someone who would love him the way he loved her. She would forever regret the way she acted toward him.

Barb moved on from Arnie. She saw what bringing him into her life was doing to Ophelia. She realized she needed to focus on what was left of her and O's relationship before her daughter moved out forever.

Ophelia graduated high school and moved out of the house where Barb and Mickey had raised her and Trenton. Barb threw a graduation party with the whole family there to celebrate. That was the last time the whole family was together in that house. Kate even flew in for the occasion.

"I'm proud of you, honey. Now get out there and show the world what you're made of," she told Ophelia.

It was finally time for the next chapter of her life to begin. Though she would never leave Texas, she was ready to leave Dallas and her adolescence behind.

9

OPHELIA'S DEPRESSION

W hat a relief it was to be pouring the last of the Lexapro down the sink drain. Ophelia felt strong and determined as ever. "You have a strength in you that most do not have," said Dr. Patel. "I hope you continue to find your happiness and peace."

O walked out of her last appointment feeling ready to make herself a better person. She was twenty-two, and she'd overcome depression. She was on her path to her own peace.

Depression is a funny thing, Ophelia thought. *It built in you one day, and you felt sadness you couldn't explain, and it grew until it took over your life. You could never understand how life could make you so sad or angry. The pain burned inside you and spread like a fire. The hole it burned in you made you feel so empty and useless inside.*

Ophelia never fully understood depression at sixteen, but she knew something was not right. She heard Barb, Kate, Dee, and Lillian talk about it endlessly. They always seemed to be making a joke out of it. But they'd lived with it their whole lives; Ophelia was just coming to terms with it for the first time. They were always asking, "Which antidepressant are you trying these days?" over cocktails. Ophelia watched how the anger, hurt, and sadness had overtaken the women in her life until the depression drove many of their decisions and accounted for so many of their actions. The Harold women just lived with it as if it were an old friend.

In Ophelia's case, it didn't hit her all at once. Depression grew on O like a virus. It crept up on her over the years. Emotions, hormones, confusion, boys, and alcohol all aided the growth of the disorder. Just as she inherited the emotional sensitivity of the Harold women, she inherited the disorder too.

She never forgot the first time she hurt herself. It was a school night, and she'd stared at herself in the bathroom mirror for hours. She saw all her emptiness staring back at her. She was sixteen, and she felt the weight of sadness crouched within her. A simple blade to the arm. It wasn't about trying to take her own life—it was more about feeling something. It was the pain and torture that brought some sort of satisfaction to her. Watching her skin break open and the blood run down her arms brought some sort of conclusion to how she was feeling. It was almost as if she wanted to show herself physically the pain she was feeling mentally.

It worsened when O went away to college. Maybe the pain she'd buried deep down inside was finally growing and festering because she'd never really dealt with it. Her relationships were changing, and she felt so alone. She watched Barb and Mickey go on to remarry. Although she was happy to see her parents move on to who they were meant to be, her world was changing before her eyes, and she didn't know which way to move forward. She felt so sick. Her relationship with Barb continued to deteriorate more as she put more and more distance between them. Ophelia knew she had to take a step back and deal with herself before she could ever pick back up with Barb again.

Ophelia felt so trapped by Barb most of her life, but as she finally broke away from her mother, she grew fearful of what lay ahead for her. Could she really find the happiness she dreamed of? Why hadn't things happened for her yet? Why did she feel so alone?

Dee and Chuck moved to South America to start an adventure of their own. Ophelia's connection to Dee waned after she'd grown past childhood, and she'd never managed to reestablish it as a teen or young adult. Dee was Barb's biggest supporter, and watching Barb and Ophelia at odds with each other was never easy on her. She always ended up siding with Barb if it came to taking sides. Dee understood the pain her sister was in, but she couldn't begin to figure out the puzzle of Ophelia.

Ophelia went home over Christmas break the year she turned nineteen. At odds with her mother, she opted to stay with Mickey in the house they'd grown up in. Trenton was home, as well. Ophelia and Trenton had both gone out for a wild night of drinking with the old high school friends. The night ended with Trenton and Ophelia challenging each other to a game of kings with a few other friends in their pool house.

It was the night before O was scheduled to drive back

to college. Severely intoxicated, she stumbled back into her bedroom to retire for the night. Overwhelmed and out of control, she went into her bathroom and took a blade to both of her arms. She sliced and diced her skin until it was completely covered in blood. She watched the blood ooze and fall into the bathroom sink, her mascara running down her face.

Ophelia looked at herself in the mirror and saw an empty, broken girl looking back at her. She hated the girl in the mirror. How had she become so weak? She was determined to put an end to it. She felt a certainty bloom inside her: this was the last she would ever cut herself. But the severe amount of alcohol she had drank made it impossible for her to stop the bleeding. O did the best she could, but her head hurt from all the alcohol; finally she was forced to lie down. She stumbled into her room, put on her black sorority fleece sweater to hide her arms, and passed out, completely forgetting about what she had just done.

Mickey woke her the next morning, saying he would make her breakfast before she made the drive back to college. Disheveled and not fully aware of what was going on, U felt an aching in her arms she'd never felt before. She's raised her sleeves to find both arms caked in dried blood. It was a sight she would never forget. Her arms looked like they'd been through a shredder, and her head ached from the cheap Yellow Tail wine she'd inhaled with Trenton the night before.

Ophelia washed her arms of the dried blood and did her best to conceal the wounds with a long-sleeve shirt. As she walked across the house to the kitchen, she could smell the migas Mickey was making. She was halfway across the living room when she collapsed. Seeing stars and out of breath, Ophelia did her best to pull herself together and get to the kitchen.

"Rough night?" asked Mickey.

"You could say that," replied O.

"Well, Trenton hasn't made it up. My guess is you won't see him before you go."

Trenton always slept through breakfast these days. He got away with staying out till five in the morning and sleeping until three the next day. Ophelia never understood this; she felt pressured to be up and going every day of her life. Trenton made it look so easy to be careless.

The drive back to college seemed to last an eternity. She'd kept this sadness she carried a secret for many years. She'd mentioned it to Barb once. Barb believed her, but she wasn't sure what to do. Her mother had her own problems to deal with, so dealing with Ophelia's was not top of her mind.

Ophelia returned to college and stayed silent for many weeks. She attended class but then shut herself up in her room, hoping she'd magically crawl out of the hole she was in. It felt like she was stuck in a deep cave with no way out; she couldn't even find the means to make a decision to come out. O was terrified and confused and didn't understand how to pull herself out of the gloom.

She finally called Mickey one night, crying and telling him she couldn't go on.

"Daaaddy," Ophelia said in a soft voice.

Mickey could feel how terrified she was. It took everything in him to stay calm, to be the strong man he knew she needed.

"What is it O?" he replied slowly and softly. He knew the sound of that voice. He'd heard it in Barb too often.

Ophelia began to sob. She had barely left her room in weeks except to go to class. Her friends didn't know what was wrong with her. "I can't . . . I can't escape my thoughts. I'm so miserable, and I can't even begin to explain it." Ophelia just sobbed. "I just don't know if I can go on."

Mickey knew his daughter wasn't okay. She hadn't been okay for a long time, but this was rock bottom, and he knew he had to pull her out. Mickey and Barb both had seen a sadness festering in their daughter for the past couple of years. The happy girl they'd raised lost her smile and sparkle many years before.

"Okay, O. I need you to calm down and go to sleep. We will handle this in the morning."

It was the middle of the night on a Thursday. Ophelia hung up and cried herself to sleep, just as she had so many nights before. She didn't know how to move forward or where her life was leading. The future terrified her in so many ways. Would she ever truly be happy? She longed to fulfill her life in every single way, but she lived in so much fear of moving forward.

Henry, Ophelia's boyfriend, was away studying abroad that summer but never missed the opportunity to tell her how much he missed her. Even their relationship wasn't enough for her to escape the loneliness she felt. Ophelia hadn't responded to him in a while. This was too big for her, and he couldn't save her. She was lost and broken; she felt she had nowhere to turn. Ophelia dozed off, dreaming of a better life.

The next morning she woke to a flight confirmation and an email from Mickey. "A ticket home. Come see us. Hang on, sweetie. I'm here for you always. Love you, Dad."

O was on a plane home to Mickey in a matter of hours.

Upon Ophelia's return home, Mickey had Trenton and Amy there waiting.

In hindsight, Ophelia saw it was this weekend that saved her life. It was a weekend spent with the ones she loved and trusted the most, the people who loved her back. Amy didn't say much; she just held O's hand the way she always did. By the end, Ophelia felt her spirits lifting. On the last day, when it was just Mickey and O, they had a long talk about the road ahead.

"I know you don't like therapy or talking to someone but, sweetie, this is beyond you, me, and the rest of the family," said Mickey.

Mickey and Barb made Ophelia go to a therapist when they first split up. Ophelia didn't like it. The guy was a fossil to her, and she wasn't ready to open up with a man she was uncomfortable with. This was also the therapist who was working with Mickey and Barb, so it never felt right.

"It's time for you to sit down and work through what-ever it is deep down in there that's bugging you."

O nodded.

"You're also going to see a psychiatrist," explained Mickey. "I'm lining up the best doctors to take care of you.

You've got to work this out and nip it in the bud. Life is a beautiful thing, and you have to embrace it. "

Mickey had gone through this for years with Barb. He'd watched it consume Lillian's life. He'd seen it turn Kate, Dee, and Barb against each other. He was determined not to let depression take his daughter down, as well. And now Ophelia was finally able to admit she had a problem. Mickey was damn determined to fix this for his daughter.

"This is not going to ruin your life like it has theirs. Not my daughter."

Ophelia would educate herself on her mood and feelings. Why had she felt this way? She had a good life. But she would learn that depression is one of the most difficult things in the world to try to explain to people. They want to know what it is that's making you so sad and why you can't just get over it and move on. It affects everyone differently, and even the strongest can't fight it off at times. It's how you deal with it that allows you to live with or overcome it. Ophelia took Mickey's lead, agreeing to whatever he decided for her.

She returned to college and her boyfriend, Henry. Henry, a pre-med major, thought he was an expert in all things medicine. He was determined to fix Ophelia too. They had met at a party his fraternity threw. Henry was older and found Ophelia to be beautiful and hilarious. One night when Ophelia drank one too many sangrias, he sat beside her, holding her hair while she threw up. He lay next to her that night as she passed out, never leaving her side and applying a cool, damp cloth to her forehead all night. That night set the tone for their relationship:

Ophelia spiraling into a complete mess and Henry doing all he could to put her back together.

Ophelia liked Henry, but it wasn't enough. She always thought he liked her enough for the both of them. Henry wanted to marry young and start a family, and he fell for the beautiful Ophelia the moment he laid eyes on her. He thought he could make her into the perfect wife he'd always been searching for. He wanted a real life with Ophelia, but as he grew to know her, he saw her depression as a setback. He would do all he could to fix her. Ophelia, meanwhile, was in a haze she couldn't escape from, and the thought of being someone's wife terrified her to no end. How could she possibly love another human being when she didn't even love herself?

After picking her up from her sessions with Anna, the psychologist, and Dr. Patel, the psychiatrist, Henry drove Ophelia to the CVS to pick up her first prescription of Lexapro. Henry counseled O on the side effects and how she probably shouldn't drink while on the prescription. Ophelia just nodded and stared out the window on the way home as Henry rambled on about the marvels of medicine and how he'd pull her through this. He needed his perfect girlfriend and life, and Ophelia knew deep down she'd never be able to be that for him.

Despite battling depression, Ophelia was still a sorority girl and had no interest in Henry counseling or fathering her on how to live her life. She would take the prescription, but she was still going to live her life. Ophelia was stubborn and hard-headed when it came to dealing with her depression at first. She never wanted to be told what to do. She took enough direction from Mickey, but she definitely didn't need it from Henry.

She felt alone. How could she talk to anyone about all this? She was embarrassed for feeling this way. She called the only person she thought may understand.

"Is my heart supposed to be beating this fast?" asked Ophelia.

"What are you taking again? Lexapro? Hmmmmm, Lexapro didn't really do the trick for me. I'm a true believer in Zoloft. But it worked for Lillian pretty well," said Barb over the phone. "You know, just take it easy. Pills are great, though, right? Already noticing a difference, aren't ya? Well, Bill and I are off to France. Enjoy school. Love ya!"

Barb had remarried that year, as had Mickey. O's parents had both finally found the love of their life. And, in a way, they were starting new chapters in their lives with their kids gone and a chance to start fresh.

Ophelia hung up immediately and called Kate.

"Hello? Is that you, bug? What's been going on? Barb's going all ape shit because she says you've been having a tough time. You okay, kiddo?" said Kate.

"Getting there. Started Lexapro this week, and it's making my heart pound and I'm all shaky," Ophelia said softly.

"Really? That's odd. Well, I'm sure you're just getting used to it. If you don't feel better soon, you may want to change prescriptions. Listen, bug, I have to run. It's apparently Utah Founder's Day, and the damn liquor store is closed, so I have to figure something else out. Love you. Come see me and come ski this winter!"

Kate had also started a new chapter in her life. She'd left her high-profile job in San Francisco behind for her new life in Utah. She had built a very successful career that ate up the majority of her time.

Kate's course in life changed the day she was called for jury duty in San Francisco. She was forty-five and accomplished, but she had no real happiness to show for it. She went into jury duty and took her number and waited, feeling frantic. Her blackberry was buzzing nonstop as the work emails piled up. The deal with Motorola was coming through, and she wasn't at the office to get it. The officer called the next pool of jurors one through thirty. Kate looked down and realized she was number seven. As they shuffled into the courtroom, the judge gave his speech to the jurors about it being a privilege and a right for a US citizen to serve on a jury. The judge then concluded by saying if there were any reason why someone could not serve on the jury, they should see him privately; but work was not an excuse. Kate was the first one in front of the judge.

"There's no way I can serve on this jury," explained Kate.

"And why not, young lady?" replied the judge.

"You don't understand. I manage 10 million in sales for Fox in San Francisco. My income relies on being there for my clients day in and day out. My entire life hangs on my income each year. If I'm not in the office taking care of the clients, I lose it all," Kate explained. "I work eighty hours a week, and if I miss a day, it sets me back even more hours."

The judge lowered his glasses and took a long, hard look at a trembling Kate.

"Young lady, I'm going to let you off because it sounds like you have your hands full. But can I give you a piece of advice? You need to find a better life," the judge said.

Six months later, Kate pulled up to the condo she'd purchased with Lillian several years earlier tucked away in the mountains of Park City, Utah. Her Pathfinder was completely full of all her clothes and her two labs fighting over the front seat. The moving truck wouldn't be far behind with the rest of her things. She had quit her job and left her life in San Francisco behind. It was a new chapter for Kate. And like Barb, she was moving on too.

Meanwhile, Ophelia kept battling her demons. Balancing antidepressants and being a social college student came with its price. While the parties were fun, the emotions would sometimes run high. Ophelia often took it out on the guy in her life, a pattern she hadn't managed to shake.

"I care for you, O, but do you even care about me?" Henry asked one night. Henry had been at home studying and O had been out with girlfriends at another fraternity party. O felt nothing these days. She only knew how to go out and have a good time with friends and try to forget about everything else going on around her. But it never worked. She was standing in the middle of the fraternity party when she made the call to Henry to come pick her up. She passed out in his truck while he drove her to his house and put her into his bed. The next morning he was wide awake, sitting up in bed next to her, working on a paper on his laptop. She just laid next to him and stared at the wall with her back to him. There was nothing in her. She felt the pills had sucked away her soul. She wasn't unhappy or happy. She couldn't feel a single thing.

"O, you can't keep on like this. You don't always have to be the life of the party. You're dealing with a lot emotionally while also trying to be the sorority superstar. You're never going to get well at this rate," he said, pounding away on his laptop. "I care about you a lot, and I see the pain in you. But, seriously, do you even care about me or our future?"

Ophelia just lay there and stared into space. She felt nothing; she had nothing to say. That was the way Ophelia handled life; she never talked about what bothered her. She just forged ahead, trying to get through her college years.

"O. O! Talk to me," Henry screamed.

"I'm not doing this right now." Ophelia got up and called her roommate to come get her.

"One day, O, I'm not going to be around to pick you up off the ground!" he said as she walked out the door. And he meant it.

Henry despised the way Ophelia needed to be the life of the party. He had fun when they were out with their friends, but by the time they got home, Ophelia was throwing up from the mix of alcohol and antidepressants or shutting down emotionally and distancing herself from him.

And Ophelia despised Henry at times, wanting nothing to do with him. She knew that was wrong. She was the one pushing him away when he was only trying to help. He didn't deserve that. He was a good guy.

Ophelia lost Henry to her carelessness and drunken emotion. The worst of it was that Ophelia felt nothing when she just wanted to feel everything. Ever since she was a little girl, she wanted the man of her dreams, the knight in shining armor to take her in his arms and carry her away, leaving all her troubles behind. Here she had another man willing to give her the world, but still she felt nothing.

How could Ophelia have known she had to love herself first before any man would be allowed to love her? That was a lesson she wouldn't learn for many years to come. She wasn't ready to be the woman that Henry needed. He couldn't fix her. Only Ophelia could fix herself. She just didn't know how.

Eventually, they agreed to end things. And Ophelia saw in time that was for the best. She needed to be alone. She was determined to focus on her therapy and make it to graduation. Though she enjoyed her college years, she was ready to start her life. She was ready to set out on the path to achieving the life of independence she'd always dreamed of. She was too young to handle everything that had happened to her. It had aged her so quickly. But it also had catapulted her into learning to work hard for the life she wanted.

A fire began to ignite in Ophelia. A fire that warmed her ambition to be the woman she wanted to become. She always had the power within her, but she had just lost herself for a while. Though she hadn't found herself entirely yet, she knew she was on the road to recovery. And there were many more adventures ahead. She no longer felt the need to harm herself. She had a life that was worth building. Ophelia still had so much to overcome, but she finally believed she was a work in progress.

By the time Ophelia weaned herself from the Lexapro, she felt more in control of herself and her emotions. She didn't need a drug anymore to control what was inside her. Pulling into her driveway, Ophelia saw clearly for the first time how much she had to be thankful for. That her path away from Henry had gifted her the strength to stand on her own. That she had a father like Mickey with the love and strength to put her on the road to healing.

Yes, she would be forever grateful to Mickey for saving her life. He had heard her call of struggle and fought to pull her out of it. And she saw now that she had his confidence inside her too. She could become the woman she had always aspired to be.

THE CRAZY HEART

O phelia's adult years arrived. This was now her time. But navigating adulthood was not as easy a transition as Ophelia envisioned for herself. She didn't have the slightest clue where to go. But it was the time in her life that she had been trying to fast forward to since she was a child.

Her relationship with Barb was as strained as ever. As part of her recovery and road to finding happiness, Ophelia was learning to love Barb from afar. Ophelia didn't want to drive away her mother. But she learned she was much happier without the drama in her life. She no longer blamed Barb; she just wanted peace between them. So it was easier to take their relationship in doses these days.

Her relationship with Lillian was changing too. The strain between Ophelia and Barb drove a wedge between Lillian and Ophelia. Lillian hated to watch Ophelia and Barb drift apart. As O grew older, Lillian didn't agree with many of her life choices. In turn, Ophelia saw a much more negative side to Lillian and disagreed with her pessimistic view on life. The cherished relationship they once had would never be the same again.

Ophelia was beginning to cut negativity in her life. It was the only way she knew how to move forward. Overcoming depression was no small feat, but the real battle was ensuring she never went back to those dark places again. She had to find ways to surround herself with what made her happy. Sometimes it took stepping away from the current situation for a while to heal before returning.

Though she'd made huge strides forward with the changes she was making in her life, something deep in O broke every once in a while. She fought so hard at times to maintain the strength she had built—to be the powerful woman she knew she could be. But in her weaker moments, she sometimes collapsed. Her emotions still got the best of her every now and again. She said things she'd later regret or react in ways she didn't intend to.

The constant drinking and partying didn't help Ophelia either. It was the downfall of yet another of O's relationships. This time with a man named Seth, a man she fell in love with and probably the only man who accepted her and the struggles she faced. He would come to learn the good and the bad and love her for all of it.

They'd known each other in high school as acquaintances but were never truly friends, and Seth came back into her life in her early twenties. Seth was older, a few years ahead of Ophelia, and was friends with Trenton. Ophelia was constantly in and out of relationships up until the day Seth walked back into her life. She'd always admired him from afar, though. She'd never expected him to come back into her life the way he did. When they met again, it was through Trenton and a few other mutual friends.

Seth approached her in his charming way, but he was a little timid when he spoke to her. He was just a few inches taller than Ophelia and had stalky brown hair and brown eyes. Ophelia loved his laugh; it always made her giggle. Seth spent the next several weeks doing everything he could to win Ophelia over. When she fell for him, she couldn't help feeling he was the man she had been waiting for in many ways. He saw her for who she was—the girl fresh out of college—but he also saw her potential to be the woman she dreamed of becoming.

Seth made O feel safe; falling for him was so easy and comfortable. It was like they were meant to be. He was one of the smartest men she'd ever met, and she admired his strength and ambition.

Ophelia would never forget the day Seth told Trenton about the two of them, hoping to get his blessing. Seth didn't have the greatest reputation when it came to women. Seth was hosting a party at his house and had invited many of their friends. Ophelia and Seth had kept the relationship under wraps but decided it was time to come out to the world.

"I don't want to hide this anymore," Seth said, cupping Ophelia's face in his hands. The two were hiding in a room away from the rest of the party. "I'm going to talk to Trenton and tell him about us. I'm ready for our relationship to be out there."

Ophelia planted a big kiss on Seth. "Okay. I'm ready.

Good luck." Ophelia followed behind Seth as he went off in search of Trenton.

Seth pulled him into the room with him and Ophelia. Trenton had been enjoying himself and the party all day and was not prepared for the serious conversation that came next.

"Trenton. We need to talk. I'm dating your sister, and it's pretty serious. I need to know you're okay with this," Seth said very quickly.

"I'm sorry. You're what? Are you out of your mind?" Trenton yelled as he stared between Seth and Ophelia. "Ophelia, no! Do you know what you're getting into?"

"Look, Trenton, it's different with O. I know I don't have the best track record, but know my intentions are good. I'd never hurt her. I'm in love with her," Seth explained calmly.

Ophelia's heart melted, and she reached for Seth's hand as she stared back at her brother.

"Whatever. Don't come crying to me—either of you— when it doesn't work out. This is a disaster waiting to happen," Trenton said and stormed off.

"Well, that went well," Seth said as he turned to give O a hug.

"He'll come around, I promise," O said. And Trenton did. He grew to be a big supporter of their relationship.

Seth supported Ophelia's ambition and her battle to find happiness. He constantly pushed her to be better and to live her happiest life. He knew the potential she had, and he saw her fire to succeed. He hated to see her in her sad moments and would do everything in his power to bring her back to happiness. In turn, she adored his ambition, as well. He was the first man who had come into Ophelia's life that she actually saw a real future with. She would have married him if he asked.

He made love to her in the best way possible. For the first time in her life, Ophelia actually enjoyed physical intimacy. Intimacy with Seth was the icing on the cake to their relationship. It wasn't a power he had over her; he fulfilled all her desires. Their emotional and physical connection was like no other. He made her feel loved in every possible way.

But though Ophelia had achieved so much, she was far from whole. There was still a battle within her, waged between the woman she could be and the woman she was trying to run away from. Slowly, Seth watched the woman he loved disappear into the battlefield. In the moments when Ophelia slipped in and out of darkness, that perfect woman Seth had fallen for turned against him. She said things she didn't mean and damaged him in ways neither of them could repair. When she realized this, she ran for the hills, trying to get as far away from him as she could.

And she hadn't yet broken free from her reliance on alcohol and the need to numb herself to lose control and forget everything. Ophelia hit a low point on her twenty-fourth birthday. It was a night she would never be allowed to forget.

Lying on the ground of the Crate and Barrel parking lot, Ophelia couldn't move. Her black strappy wedge was completely misplaced from her foot and wrapped around her ankle, hanging like an ornament. Her arm ached from breaking her fall onto the pavement. A small pool of blood formed beneath her elbow. Her head spun from all the tequila shots she had taken with Trenton just an hour before. It was her twenty-fourth birthday, and she lay on the pavement alone, sobbing, and looking up into the starry sky above her.

What am I doing with myself? Who am I becoming? Ophelia demanded of herself. Her phone lay next to her. She thumbed several text messages to Seth; she'd been angry with him earlier, but now she needed him. She needed him to rescue her just like he always did. She had grown to rely on him to pull her out when things went dark.

The night had started off in such a lovely way. Ophelia's closest friends had planned the whole event. Mexican food had always been a tradition of O's birthdays celebrated with her friends. She'd walked into the restaurant to find her nine closest girlfriends and Amy, a complete fajita station bar, and several pitchers of margaritas. It was a dinner for just the girls. The guys would meet up with them later. O hadn't seen much of her friends lately. She'd spent many of her days, nights, and weekends slaving away at her job, hoping to continue to prove herself to move forward. On her free nights, she was thankful to spend time with those she loved.

Tonight she planned to have fun. Tonight she'd forget about work, about the problems she had with Seth, about the life she was striving to build, the bills she had to pay. Tonight she'd drink it all away. It was loud in the restaurant, but the girls had decorated a small private area. The table was filled with pink cupcakes that O's friend Stacey had spent the day baking for her. It was her night to celebrate.

"To our girl, Ophelia!" said Amy, raising her glass. "We're all so gosh darn proud of you. You have one of the biggest hearts in the world, and we all love you for it. You're the truest and most loyal friend in the world. Happy birthday, baby girl!" The girls all sloshed their margarita glasses together as O looked around the room, feeling so fortunate for the love that surrounded her.

A couple of hours later, they were at Ophelia's favorite bar. The music roared and the girls were all dancing. They'd taken a tequila shot when they arrived, O's favorite. Trenton, Seth, and several of the other guys arrived.

"Shots all around for my baby sister!" yelled Trenton as he took her into a bear hug. "Did you talk to Mom?" he asked. She stared back at him and nodded. She'd spoken to Barb briefly that day, calling to thank her for the card and money she'd sent. O took several more shots of tequila. Seth joined in on the fun but watched O from the corner of his eye.

They had broken up for the twelfth time. O honestly didn't know if they were together that night or not. Seth was growing tired of Ophelia, and she knew it. He wanted his confident, beautiful girlfriend back, the one who would fight for the life she wanted. But he wasn't ready to be the man she needed him to be. He was still young and determined to live his life. He laughed with Trenton and the other guys. He seemed like such a child to her at times. She so badly needed him to be the strong man to take care of her.

And after seven shots of tequila and several spins around the dance floor later, O turned into another person.

The monster inside her became outraged. She blamed Seth for not being a good boyfriend to her. She blamed Trenton for her issues with herself and her family. And with that she stormed out of the bar. Tears welling up inside, the flood gates opened and she sobbed and stumbled home on the walk back to her apartment. It was extremely hot on that summer night, and sweat ran down her face that tasted like salt and tequila. She was crossing the Crate and Barrel parking lot back into her apartment complex when she tripped on her shoe and skidded across the asphalt. Her skin tore open and blood pulsed out of her arm and leg.

"Ophelia! Oh my God!" yelled Amy. O looked up some time later to see Amy running toward her. "Are you all right?" Trenton and Seth were not far behind her.

"Jesus Christ, O! There's blood everywhere. What the hell is the matter with you?" yelled Trenton. He was angry. He hated seeing her like this. His perfect, sweet sister was completely disheveled and not in her right mind.

O still couldn't move. She didn't know if it was the tequila going straight to her head or the pain from her arm that paralyzed her.

Seth was furious and Ophelia would barely say a word. She was a mess, and he couldn't do anything but stare down at her. He scooped her up off the ground in one swift movement and carried her across the parking lot and into the building. The blood pouring from her arm seeped into his white linen shirt. Amy and Trenton followed behind them. Amy was crying, as she always did when O fell apart.

Seth turned on the shower and laid O in the bathtub. He removed her bloodstained white dress and threw it onto the bathroom floor. She sat in silence as Seth washed the blood off of her and determined where the bleeding was coming from. She had punctured a hole in the bottom of her elbow. It looked as if someone had taken a spoon and scooped out a chunk of her elbow.

"Damn it, Ophelia. I know you're upset. I'm not sure what the hell about. But you can't go running off by yourself like this," Seth said, seeing the state her elbow was in. Trenton was yelling in the living room while Amy tried to call him down. He was angry at how Ophelia had behaved that night. And he was terrified when she ran off alone.

Ophelia could only sit there, watching the chaos she'd created swirling around her. She was completely in shock, and her whole body ached. Seth wrapped up her elbow. He couldn't get the bleeding to stop, so he continued to put pressure on it. He wrapped her in a towel and carried her to her bed. O sat and stared at the wall while Seth dug through her chest of drawers looking for pajamas.

She couldn't look at him. She was too ashamed by how the night had played out. Too ashamed of what they had done to each other.

The chatter from Amy and Trenton finally stopped, and Seth put her in a T-shirt and wrapped her elbow again. Ophelia was so tired, and her head felt heavy as she crawled into bed. Seth followed and lay down beside her, still putting pressure on her elbow until they both drifted off to sleep.

O woke the next morning with her head in throbbing pain and her elbow caked in dried blood. She swore to herself she'd take control of her drinking. She had made plans to see Barb that day and got into the car when she came to pick her up. Before O could even explain her current hangover and bandage over her arm, she realized Barb already knew.

Trenton had called and told Barb everything, and Barb insisted on picking O up later that morning to take her to lunch. She spent most of it lecturing Ophelia or casting stones at her behavior from the night before. Ophelia always felt it was unfair for Barb to judge her. Sometimes she just needed her mother to be a friend, to offer understanding. These were things she could never talk about with Barb. It was always her fault somehow.

Not long after this episode, Ophelia ran off to Utah to spend time with Kate. She needed to escape to heal herself and find the answers to move on. Seth and Ophelia agreed to take time apart. During her time in Utah, Ophelia learned that Kate had fallen in love again, but this time she could tell something was different.

"I'm seeing someone. It's pretty serious," Kate told Ophelia over a couple of shots of sake. "I think I'm in love with him."

"Okay, I've been here for three days and you're just now telling me this? Name? Who is he? What's his story?" O asked.

"He's younger, and he's a bartender. He makes me laugh harder than anyone I've ever met," Kate gushed.

She seemed so happy; Ophelia could see it written all over her face. And she beamed when she took Ophelia to the bar where Calvin worked. Kate got so drunk that night she fell off her barstool. "And you're worried about me?" Ophelia teased. Ophelia had never seen Kate smile the way she did when she was with Calvin. After many years alone, her auntie had found *the one*.

Ophelia returned home, vowing to turn over a new leaf and make her career front and center in her life. And she did, but her personal life slipped away as she focused her energy on building a career. It was the only thing she knew how to do right.

Ophelia was at a fork in her career path. Even though she and Seth were no longer together, she always relied on him to help her with important decisions. Seth seemed content to come over and let O talk things out. Though they were not together, O still leaned on him.

On this particular night, Seth brought over a bottle of wine, and Ophelia cooked dinner. They talked through her career choices, and he helped her come to a conclusion. Before they knew it, they were making out on the couch just like they used to until O couldn't do it anymore. She began to cry hysterically.

"Seth, you have to make this right between us. Why can't we get this together? We can't do this to each other anymore," Ophelia said as she sat on the end of her bed with her face in her hands.

Seth bent down in front of her.

"Hey, look at me," he said, cupping her face in his hands. "I know you, Ophelia—probably better than most. I'm so damn proud of the woman you are becoming. I also know the man you need. I know the man you deserve, and I can't be that man to you. I'm your biggest supporter. I'll always have your back, O. Anything you need, I'll be here. But you need to move on from me."

He kissed her goodbye and left. He was done trying to put Ophelia back together when she fell apart and no longer wanted to be by her side. It was years before they spoke again.

Seth was the hardest one for Ophelia to get over. He was the only man she'd ever envisioned marrying and having children with. And now he was gone.

The reckless nights of her early twenties slowed and came to an end as Ophelia slowly learned to overcome her depression for good. Her simplest but most profound lesson was that happiness was not something given; it was a choice.

Ophelia learned after so many years in pain that she had to actively wake up and choose to make herself happy every day. Day by day, she learned to surround herself with the people and things that lit her up. And inch by inch, she moved toward wholeness.

IS IT YOUR FAULT OR MINE?

Her career was beginning to take off, and Ophelia was rising through the ranks. She was working harder than she ever had. She'd barely found the time to make it to Kate's wedding out in Napa. She hadn't spent much time with Kate lately. Like everyone else, it seemed Kate had moved on and started her new life too.

Ophelia was the maid of honor at Kate and Calvin's wedding. She watched as Kate walked toward real happiness. She stood by Kate's side, happy to see Calvin staring at Kate with adoring eyes. After all the years Kate had walked a lonely path, she deserved the love she found in Calvin.

Ophelia thought of the toast she'd given at Kate's rehearsal dinner. She could remember every word with unusual clarity.

"Tonight I raise my glass to my dearest auntie. Finding love is one of life's greatest gifts. I've watched you and admired you for so many years. Your beauty, strength, and resilience make you a woman I look up to. You've never settled and always pursued the best for yourself. I knew Calvin was the one for you from the moment you told me about him—that night I came to Utah. I knew just by the look on your face and the slight tears in your eyes that everything was just as it should be. Life has a funny way of working itself out. All your choices and the paths you've walked have led you to this very moment and into this man's arms. The man you were made to be with. And, Calvin, I've known you for only a short time, but I've grown to love you as an uncle so quickly. Thank you for loving my Kate the way she deserves to be loved. You're marrying one of the greatest women I've ever known. Be kind to one another. I wish you two nothing but good health and happiness as you make new memories together."

Kate's old flame Peter officiated the wedding. He'd kept his promise to remain Kate's loyal friend. He'd grown to love Calvin, as well. He had moved on and was married now, but his friendship with Kate was as strong as ever.

The holidays would come quickly that year, and although she'd watch Kate extend into another family, she couldn't help but notice that the original family she knew began to drift apart.

Barb barely got an invitation to the wedding. Her relationship with Kate continued to be a source of tension for both of them. But Barb was happy to see her little sister finally settle down. It was a joint effort between Trenton and Ophelia to keep Barb from making a scene. Lillian seemed oblivious to the drama, just happy to see that all her daughters had found love.

Barb and O barely spoke at the wedding. They barely spoke at all these days. It angered Barb, and she lashed out, telling Ophelia she'd turned into a real bitch. Ophelia told Barb not to bother setting a place for her at Christmas. There was still so much she needed to work through on her own, and she wasn't ready to let Barb back in yet.

She was happy to get back home to her routine and feeling so peaceful about gliding through the upcoming holiday without seeing her mother. Then, a few days before Christmas, Ophelia received the email from Bill. Barb had married Bill in Italy years before. Ophelia did not attend the wedding. She barely knew her stepdad, so she was in shock to see his email in her inbox.

Dear Ophelia

I don't know what your deal is, but you need to learn to have some sort of relationship with your mother. Your cockiness is not appreciated. You're not better than anyone. I'm over it and the way you treat my wife. You're breaking her heart, and I won't have it anymore. You need to figure this out and make the effort to build a relationship again.

Best,
  Bill

Ophelia honestly didn't know what Bill was talking about. What had Barb told him? She barely spoke to Barb these days anyway. She got on the phone and read the email to

Mickey, hoping to get some perspective. He was not happy with Bill's meddling.

"I'm going to write him back, Daddy. This isn't fair," Ophelia said.

"Do you what you think is best, but just be factual and to the point. You don't need to make it any more dramatic than it already is."

After she hung up with Mickey, Ophelia sat down and crafted her response.

Dear Bill,

Thank you for your concern. I understand where you are coming from. You're her husband, and the last person that you want to see upset is your wife. I'm going to ask you to please stay out of this, though. I have my reasons for staying distant as that is the best choice for the sake of my happiness at this time. I've been called a "bitch" my entire life. While I know she doesn't mean it and does love me, it doesn't make it right. Please respect my choices at this time. Hopefully one day we can come together.

Xoxo,

  O

Ophelia never heard back from Bill, and they never spoke of the incident again. The holidays came and went. Ophelia couldn't help thinking how much the holiday season had changed for her over the years. She thought back to the happy memories of her childhood, when her mother's house was filled with laughter and the bantering and bickering of her aunts. It used to fill her with such warmth, so many dreams. Now it just depressed her. Through her adult eyes, she could see all too clearly how the darkness in her family had warped everyone and everything. Sometimes she felt there was nothing to hope for, nothing to feel warm about in this season. She welcomed the passing of that Christmas season.

New Years, though, was something altogether different. Ophelia found many reasons to hope once the new year rolled around. She hoped things would get better in the months to follow.

Several weeks later, the Super Bowl was in town, and it was one of the coldest weekends Dallas had seen in quite some time. The city was completely frozen over. Mickey was in town and was taking Ophelia to dinner that night.

"Dad, is this normal?" asked O.

"Is what normal, princess?" replied Mickey as he grabbed a piece of sushi from the center of the table with a fork. Ophelia smiled, loving the way Mickey always ate his sushi with a fork.

By the time she replied, the smile had disappeared. "I'm twenty-six, and I'm not really sure if I ever want to get married. I mean, what is love anyway?" Ophelia was losing faith in the concept of marriage, doubting there was such a thing as happily ever after. Even though she'd seen so much love blooming around her, she no longer believed it was possible for everyone. Maybe she was marked with the curse of never being able to have this.

. . .

Her thoughts were constantly busy with work, but her train wreck of a back-and-forth relationship with Garrett lingered in the background and she was begging for understanding. They'd known each other since they were kids and had always been great friends. Garrett had casually strolled back into Ophelia's life, and they'd somehow fallen into this complicated love story. They cared a great deal about each other, but were too troubled to take care of one another. When Ophelia wasn't working, she always ended up in a bar drinking her sorrows away with Garrett.

He was like Ophelia in many ways—a sad soul, obsessed with his career and fighting for happiness. They both knew how to throw themselves into work. Success was a high priority in both of their lives. Ophelia found herself running away from him over and over again, only to come crawling back.

Mickey's answer sounded wise, but Ophelia found she couldn't concentrate on the words. She thought of the night she reconnected with Garrett at a friend's wedding. They'd spent the next year hanging out as friends until Garrett told her how he felt about her.

"Ophelia, when you walked into that church that night for the wedding, you had me. I knew you'd walked back into my life for a reason," he'd said.

Ophelia only registered terror. She cared for him deeply, but she also knew he was just as screwed up as she was. Losing both of his brothers, and suffering a painful previous relationship, had aged Garrett in many ways. It also caused him to give up a lot of his hope and faith in others.

Ophelia, still trying to climb her way up in her career

and figure out residual feelings for Seth, didn't really know what love or feelings meant anymore. Garrett and Ophelia became an escape for each other, but neither was strong enough to take the lead. She'd spent a year and half of recklessness with Garrett. A roller coaster of emotion and exhaustion, fighting for something that probably was never really there to begin with. She knew he wasn't the man for her, but she couldn't escape him either.

Mickey set his fork down and took a sip of wine. Ophelia snapped out of her thoughts and looked into his eyes as he said, "Ophelia, one day love is going to hit you with an arrow. And when that arrow strikes, you're going to be paralyzed. But you're also going to finally feel whole and know you wouldn't do anything to replace that feeling."

Mickey's words hit her with striking clarity. She understood she and Garrett were over. They weren't right for each other, and they never would be.

Mickey would tell her later on that his biggest regret was leaving her behind that year he left Barb. He realized later on it was the time she probably needed him the most.

"I should have been there for you, Ophelia. I didn't realize that till years later, but you needed me and I wasn't there." He left it at that, but she knew what he meant. Though it took a while, he was the one that saved her in her darkest times. And she'd always love him for that.

Later that night, she met up with Garrett at a bar. He was

drunk and careless, as usual. And she joined him with one too many drinks. They stumbled home together, laughing at dumb jokes. But when it was time to lie down, Ophelia saw through the exterior of the empty man lying beside her. He'd never be the man she needed.

Ophelia got up and stumbled home through the cold and ice. When she got to her apartment, she crawled into bed, ignoring the text messages from Garrett.

"Damnit, O! Did you run out again? Did you walk home alone? You're going to get yourself killed. You hear me?" Garrett never liked seeing Ophelia run because it brought up too much pain for him. They were so wrong for the other. Neither of them was strong enough for the other.

This was the most selfish she had ever been, Ophelia knew. She had become a perfect mess trying to navigate her way into becoming the woman she wanted to be. She knew she needed to cut ties with Garrett, but she cared about him. She worried for him and the broken man he'd become. She knew he could be so much more, but she also knew she couldn't fix him. And he couldn't fix her either.

She returned to that place inside herself, the place where she knew the truth that only she could forge her path to wholeness and strength. This was a journey she'd have to take alone. If she knew the truth, why was it so hard to bring it to life?

Several months passed before they saw each other again. Ophelia finally found the courage to put Garrett out of her life for good. It wasn't healthy anymore to be around him.

One day Ophelia was asleep in the apartment she

shared with Amy, and Amy had people in their living room. Garrett showed up unexpectedly, asking where O was. Amy pointed toward her room, shocked to see him. While Amy loved Garrett, she knew the relationship was over. Ophelia had made great strides to put him out of her life for good. Ophelia was sleeping when Garrett quietly walked into her room. She'd worked for thirteen days straight and had been looking forward to a full night of sleep. Garrett sat down next to her and gently woke her up. Ophelia was surprised to see him, barely able to make him out in the dark. He turned on the lamp as Ophelia sat up and rubbed her eyes. She was too tired and surprised to make much sense of what was happening.

"I need you to know something, Ophelia. I never want you to doubt that I cared about you. I've been in awe of you since we were kids. You are incredible. And I'm so proud of the woman you're becoming. I know good things will come for you. But it will never be right for us, not because of you but because of what we are together. Moving on is the best thing for the both of us. But please know you'll always be in my heart. I'll always admire you from afar."

Ophelia nodded. She couldn't say anything, but she knew this was goodbye for good. Garrett pulled the covers over her and kissed her forehead before letting himself out.

Garrett and Ophelia's paths crossed here and there down the road. It was always the same—they shared a tight hug, a nod, or a smile from afar. They were able to say genuinely, "I'm so happy you're doing well."

IT WAS ALL JUST A DREAM

Ophelia was walking out of a meeting when she looked down and noticed three missed calls from Dee. She hadn't spoken to her mom or the aunts in a while. Lillian's eightieth birthday was coming, and she knew it was most likely about that. She called Dee back when she got home later that night. Dee and Chuck had moved back to Texas from South America by now.

"What's going on with work these days? You're always busy," Dee said.

"Just trying to make something of myself," Ophelia replied.

"I know that, sweetie. And we're all so proud of you. But do me a favor? Don't waste away your youth dedicated to just a job. I worry about you. We all do."

Ophelia just sat silently.

"Have you spoken to your mother in a while? She says things between you all are distant still. How do we fix this?" Dee asked.

"Dee, it's not that easy. Look, I don't hate her. I just can't have the drama in my life anymore. It's better that we keep things at a distance," Ophelia explained.

She knew Dee didn't get it. That was Dee, though, always trying to fix people and bring everyone together. She was the softhearted one the family relied on.

Ophelia talked to Lillian next. Her relationship with Lillian had improved as things between her and Barb cooled off. "We're all proud of you, sweetheart, but I just hope you realize what you're doing. You're going to get all this success in life but have no one to share it with," said Lillian.

It was the curse she had hoped to avoid, but the words stuck with Ophelia for many years after.

Ophelia was beginning a new chapter. She was finally starting to make something of her career. She was becoming more and more financially stable and had the ability to buy things for herself that she wanted. She was achieving her goals professionally because that's all she knew how to do. Ophelia was so much calmer these days and felt more at ease. She was proud of the woman she was becoming.

Her health and lifestyle changes were improving, as well. She wasn't drinking as much as she used to. And she found when she wasn't drinking, she was making healthier choices that brought her a greater sense of well-being. She felt more energized. Her career had brought more travel into her life. And the journeys she took by herself changed her view of the world, her view of herself.

Ophelia sat at the hotel bar by herself in New York. She furiously tapped away at her iPad, answering one email after another. Work was the busiest it had ever been, and Ophelia welcomed the challenges being thrown her way. She'd taken a major promotion that year. At twenty-seven, she had her dream job and was on her way to buying her first home. She sipped her cold glass of chardonnay as she checked her watch for the time. It was only 4:30 p.m. Her conference had ended early, and Amy wouldn't be off work for another hour or so. She passed the time until it was time to meet her. Amy had moved to New York City in the last year. Although the distance was difficult, and not seeing her best friend every day was hard on Ophelia, she was proud of Amy. Amy left her life behind in Dallas to start a new one in New York. Luckily, Ophelia was traveling to New York more often for work, so they were able to see each other.

Ophelia checked her iPhone. Nothing. She had broken up with "what's his face" a month prior. She was having one of the best years at work, but the man in her life couldn't even show up when she was awarded one of the biggest honors she could have received. She left him shortly after. She couldn't be with a man who didn't support her. Her phone was silent these days, but she realized she welcomed that. It was good to keep focused on work. Her iPad buzzed, showing another email. This time it was from her realtor. The offer she'd made on that townhome had been accepted. She'd be a homeowner soon.

Ophelia smiled to herself as she happily drank her chardonnay at the end of the bar. *Things are looking up*, she thought. She was content with her life. When was the last time she'd been able to say that? Her rise to success empowered her to make healthier choices. And she'd accomplished it all on her own. She barely noticed the handsome bearded man staring right at her opposite the bar. She wasn't sure how long he'd been staring, but she smiled and continued to pound away on her iPad. He couldn't possibly be looking at her.

She looked up again, and this time they locked eyes.

He mouthed to her, "Can I buy you a drink?"

Ophelia blushed and nodded.

He motioned for the bartender to pour Ophelia another glass of wine as he picked up his own iPad and moved closer to sit next to O.

"I'm Nathan. Most call me Nate, though. I'm sorry, but you're very beautiful. I just had to talk to you," he said.

Ophelia blushed again. Nate had a very sophisticated look to him, unlike most men she'd been around. He looked like one of the cast from *Mad Men*. He was very polished and handsome. He took her breath away. He was the type of man she'd only dreamed of.

Ophelia learned that Nate was a CEO of an advertising agency, and he split his time between Los Angeles and New York. He was several years older than Ophelia, and she could see this man had lived well and accomplished a lot in his life already. He seemed strong and controlled, just the type of man Ophelia had been waiting for. He was gorgeous, and his eyes were so deep she felt she could get lost in them.

The couple stayed locked in conversation for the remainder of the afternoon, unable to break away as they learned all about each other. Ophelia looked down to notice a deck of cards next to Nate's iPad. She later learned he always carried these with him. Nate did card tricks and was a master magician. He blew Ophelia's mind doing trick after trick, making cards disappear and reappear and guessing the card she would pull from the deck.

The time passed quickly, and Ophelia finally had to leave to meet Amy. But Nate found her again later that night. They stayed up the entire night going all over New York until Ophelia's flight the next morning. Nate and the magic of New York City swept Ophelia away on a cloud.

Falling for Nate was so easy because he welcomed her fall. He made his intentions clear; he wanted to be with her no matter what. She had met a man she could completely surrender to. He'd swept her off her feet that night, and Ophelia could only hope that every man adored their woman the way he adored her.

Ophelia flew back home the next day to begin her life in her new home, but she talked to Nate on the phone every day for the next month. For the first time Ophelia had a strong man in her life who cared about her and supported her ambitions. He made her feel like she could take on anything.

Kate flew to Texas for Lillian's eightieth birthday party and stayed the weekend with her.

"Okay, so who's the guy? You literally cannot stop smiling." Kate nudged Ophelia.

"Just someone I met in New York. I don't know what it all means, but I've never had someone come after me the way he has. He makes me feel like the most beautiful woman in the world," Ophelia told Kate.

"Oh, sweetie, finally! I think it's great."

Ophelia's face wore a constant smile these days. She was earning the career she'd worked so hard for, was buying her new home, and had a handsome and successful man who adored and supported her every step of the way. She'd never had a man lift her up the way Nate did.

The night of Lillian's birthday party, Ophelia spent most of it sitting in the corner, observing all that was happening. Dee was overserved, trying to keep the peace between her two sisters while Barb and Kate continuously bickered with one another. Lillian grew tired of watching her daughters and just ignored them. For the first time, Ophelia noticed how odd it felt sitting back and watching her family interact with one another. She didn't feel as if she fit in anymore. While she was still connected to these women, she didn't really know anything about them anymore. Or maybe she was the one who had changed. She'd put distance between herself and them for the last few years.

The entire drive home, she sat in silence with Kate next to her.

"I'm worried about you, kiddo. What upset you so bad back there?" Kate asked.

Ophelia shrugged. She didn't know what it was, she just knew she wanted to escape. It was hard being around the family sometimes. It brought up thoughts and feelings she couldn't explain.

A week later, she was on a plane to see Nate. She couldn't wait to be with him. He had brought so much peace and happiness to her life. She felt safe knowing he was out there somewhere caring for her. On the night they finally reunited, she walked into that hotel bar to see the man she adored sitting on the couch, waiting for her with a huge smile spreading from ear to ear. She would never forget that. She fell into his arms, and it felt like they'd never been apart.

They made love that night, and Nate kissed every inch of her. He was a real man to her. He was strong and successful, and he completely worshipped her. Nate had breakfast delivered to them the next morning as they lay in bed for hours just holding one another. Three amazing days followed as they spent every moment together in the city where they'd first met. Nothing else mattered to Ophelia at that moment except Nate.

On the last night, Amy joined them, and they went out to a jazz bar. Ophelia looked to see Nate and Amy laughing and getting along, which was always the icing on the cake since Amy's opinion always mattered greatly to her. Nate pulled out his cards and showed Amy his magic tricks. She was blown away. Nate adored Ophelia and Amy's friendship. He'd never seen two women so supportive of one other.

Amy grabbed Ophelia and looked her dead in the eyes. "MARRY HIM. Seriously, O. I like this one. He has you on a pedestal. And you look at peace. It's all starting to come together for you. This is it."

Nate and Ophelia took a cab back to the hotel, Ophelia's head resting on Nate's shoulder. She had no idea how this would ever work, but she knew this was the man she wanted to be with. It all made sense. They stayed up late that night, enjoying one another's presence.

"Ophelia, you're an incredible woman. I'm so proud

and in awe of who you are. Your independence and your work ethic are so inspiring. Promise me something. Never settle for something that isn't right for you, and never let someone or something hold you back. I'm falling for you, and I adore every inch of who you are. Don't ever let a man tell you you're not good enough or keep you from pursuing your dreams. To me, you're perfect. And every man before me that wasn't there for you was an idiot."

Ophelia fell asleep in Nate's arms that night in the hotel in New York. Morning came, and it was time for O to go back to Texas. She grabbed her things and kissed the man she had come to admire so much goodbye as he lay half asleep in bed.

"Please let me know once you've made it home safely, my dear."

"I will," Ophelia said as she closed the hotel door behind her with a huge smile on her face.

That was the last time Ophelia ever saw him. She would never understand what happened. She tried desperately to reach Nate, but he seemed to vanish into thin air. He became only a memory. She thought of him from time to time, and she found herself comparing every man after him to the way he'd made her feel.

She would forever hold him in a safe place in her heart as the man who truly admired her, the one who saw her for the woman she was becoming. Ophelia comforted herself with the thought, *We'll always have New York*.

13

"I GET IT, O."

After Nate, it was a long time before Ophelia allowed a man back in her life. She focused her energy on building the home she'd purchased and making it her safe haven. And she wondered about trying to reach out to Barb again. She had always been committed to building some sort of relationship with her mother, and this felt like it might be a good time.

Bill and Barb came over after Ophelia moved in, but it didn't go as she'd hoped. Barb yelled at Ophelia for the way the house looked, listing off things she needed to do. In truth, Ophelia was no longer upset by it. She had learned not to take her mother's outbursts personally by now. Barb was who she was and didn't mean any harm. Bill just looked on as his wife put Ophelia down for the way things looked in the new home she had worked so hard to build on her own.

"Look, Mom, this is a zen household. We don't have any stress here. Let's stay positive," Ophelia said and winked at Bill. Bill spent the next several hours fixing things around O's home and helping her.

Ophelia picked up dinner for Barb and Bill that night, and the three of them sat down together to eat. Barb complained about trouble with her company and drama with her friends.

"All right, Barb, that's not positive. Let's stay positive," Bill said, winking back at O. Bill and Ophelia had begun to build a relationship by this point, and Ophelia was happy to have him on her side for once.

Before the night was over, Barb called Ophelia a bitch, just like she always did.

"You really shouldn't call your family members such ugly names," Ophelia said calmly.

"It's family. You're allowed to talk that way toward your family." Barb just chuckled, laughing it off.

"Actually, no, you're not," Bill and O said in unison.

That night on their way out, Bill grabbed Ophelia's arm and looked her dead in the eyes. "I get it now, O. And I'm so sorry. I should never have questioned your decisions back then. You're doing just fine."

Later that year, Dee and Chuck hosted the family in their home for the Christmas season celebrations. Lillian had been living with them the last several years. She started her days doing crossword puzzles with Dee in the morning. Dee had retired and was left with nothing to do but drink around the house to pass the time.

Barb called Ophelia and begged her to come have Christmas with them at Dee's that year. Ophelia was actively trying to have a relationship with Barb these days. While she knew they'd never have a real mother–daughter relationship, she did at least feel they could be friends somehow.

With the career and stress Ophelia had been feeling, she barely had time to get away, even on Christmas. Trenton and Ophelia were constantly torn between their parents during the holidays, but they always made an effort to split the time with both Barb and Mickey.

Kate and Calvin stayed away during the holidays, as usual. They had their own life and family. Ophelia was happy for Kate. After years of being alone, she had her own life.

Ophelia relented and made the trek to Dee and Chuck's. She was the last one to arrive Christmas Eve. She'd spend the entire drive a daze of her thoughts. She was lost these days, but her time alone had made her resilient at least. She was finding her happiness in not being in a relationship with any man. She was learning to love herself and focus on the good in life. But she couldn't help noticing how her nerves were set on edge as she neared the family Christmas.

Ophelia didn't know if her family's drinking habit had worsened or if she had just gotten older and was more aware now. Ophelia always envied the Christmas cheer around her. She hadn't felt that since her childhood years. There were too many bad Christmas memories in the years since. To her, Christmas had become something she had to survive each year. There were just so many memories to wade through, someone fighting or someone to drunk or something hurtful someone said.

Ophelia calmed herself on the three-hour drive by listening to an audiobook. She stopped at the convenience store before arriving to pick up a bottle of Pellegrino sparkling water and a bag of limes. Though Ophelia enjoyed her occasional glass or two of wine, drinking around her family made her cringe.

She arrived at Dee and Chuck's to be greeted by Dee at the door. "Girlfriend! You made it!" Dee yelled with her hands in the air.

Ophelia giggled. She always loved to see Dee. No matter what happened or what went wrong, Dee always had the power to forget about it and be the entertainment the family needed. Inside the house, Ophelia found the usual state of affairs. The air smelled of cigarette smoke. The animals wandered from room to room. The dogs looked for any food to eat while the cats jumped from one cat condo to the next.

Barb was on her third glass of chardonnay and was cooking up a storm. Lillian sat with Trenton, watching television with a gin and tonic in hand. Chuck and Bill were out back. Ophelia sat as the outside, slowly sipping the sparkling water she'd brought as the entire family refilled their booze.

When it was time for dinner, Barb yelled at Ophelia to set the table and then yelled at her again when she set the table incorrectly.

"Wait till we have to do the dishes!" Dee teased Ophelia as she walked by, placing the turkey in the center of her dining table.

"Dee, it is so damn hot in here," the men said as they piled into the dining room. It was a hot Christmas Day that year, and Dee and Chuck's air conditioning broke, so everyone was sweating. Dee turned on the fan, only to have dust bunnies rain down onto the table. Cleaning house was not something Dee felt like doing these days. She didn't feel like doing much of anything apart from her drinking.

Ophelia and Barb swatted the bunnies away so they wouldn't land in the food. Over dinner, as the wine was passed around, Ophelia remained sober, watching the way her family interacted. She felt like an outsider, like she was no longer part of the family that had raised her.

Trenton and Ophelia drove to Mickey's together the next day, much of the time sitting in silence.

"I get it, O. I really do. But don't give up on our mother. She means well. She just doesn't realize what she says sometimes and how it affects others," Trenton explained.

And Ophelia knew. She'd spent the last several years forgiving Barb, even though she'd never really received an apology from her mother. Her pain and anger were gone. She was who she was, and she'd never stop working on herself. She wouldn't allow herself to give up on her own life. That was one Harold family trait she wouldn't accept.

14

ON A STRAIGHT TEQUILA NIGHT

S itting, watching a pregnancy test while it calculated a result was the longest three minutes of Ophelia's life. There she was, thirty, on the verge of literally losing her mind. O's life had hit a wall in the last year, and meeting and falling instantly in love with Brandon was the cherry on top of it all. Though the career she had spent the greater part of her twenties building was slipping away from her, a new man had come into her life.

Ophelia had fallen for him instantly. Unfortunately, the rush of new love obscured the bad signs flashing brightly in front of her. Of all the love lessons in her life, this might have been the easiest for Ophelia to get up and walk away from, but her obsession with him prevented her from seeing reason. If she had known then, when she first met Brandon, what she knew now, things would have been different. She would never have taken this path. She was better and stronger than this. But she'd made her choice, and this was where it had landed her, staring at a pregnancy test and sobbing alone in her bathroom.

The three minutes were up. It was negative. A sigh of relief blew from Ophelia's quaking body. It was over and done with for good. Now she could start to put the pieces of all this behind her.

"I know it hurts, O. But you're doing the right thing. This man will never be there for you," said Kate on the phone that night as Ophelia wiped away whatever was left of her tears. It'd been two months since she'd last seen or spoke to Brandon. This was the finale for Ophelia. She could now close the door.

She knew she only had herself to blame for the mess she'd put herself through the last ten months.

And still, she questioned whether she was right to walk away. It was one of the hardest things she'd ever had to do. The signs were all there; she just hadn't paid attention to them until it was too late.

Ophelia had been drawn to Brandon in so many ways, from the moment they met. She was on an outdoor patio overlooking a Texas sunset and listening to a guitar player picking out old familiar country songs. She remembered being at peace that night as she watch the sun descend over the hills. Brandon barely talked to O; he barely even looked at her, but something in her was completely mesmerized in the way he talked and carried himself. The guy started singing along to the guitarist and playing air guitar. Ophelia was transfixed. To most people, he probably looked silly. But the way he let loose with such passion lit Ophelia up inside. She fell for him the moment she laid eyes on him. He came crashing into her life at a turning point. A time when she'd spent so many resources bettering herself. She was confident in the woman she was becoming. Ophelia knew then and there that he'd be in her life somehow; she just never realized it would be to break her heart.

It would be August when they'd spend those first few moments alone together and it would all officially begin. It would be her idea to meet for drinks that day. She had just taken a promotion from work and was in the mood to celebrate. They sat at the bar getting to know one another for the first time. They had always known each other by sight, but they had never sat down with one another until that day. Ophelia was drawn to him instantly. It was his energetic nature, his zest for life, his sense of humor, and his kindness toward everyone around him that caught Ophelia's heart. He had big ambitions and huge dreams for his life. Ophelia listened quietly as Brandon spent most of the time talking about himself and the goals he'd set out to accomplish.

The way he talked and moved reminded her of a lion. He was powerful and brave, but still so wild and untamed. He was a man who walked alone, but with his head held high. Everyone around him was drawn to him. Ophelia saw he was a natural-born leader. Even looking into his eyes, she could see so much depth. He had a long, complicated story that defied the norm. And through all his life experiences, he remained strong and kept a smile on his face and his ambitions rising.

"So, Ophelia, are you dating anyone right now?" asked Brandon, turning to look right at her.

"No, not currently," Ophelia quickly replied, her

stomach in knots. It was the truth; she'd taken a break for a long time since Nate. She hadn't been ready to put herself back out there.

Brandon turned and looked straight down at the bar and put both his hands flat on the bar table. "Well, I am. I mean it's not really serious. I don't know. I hope that's not weird. I couldn't not meet you, Ophelia. I had to be near you and get to know you," he explained.

Ophelia nodded. She was somewhat relieved. She could push all the attraction away and just focus on being his friend.

"But, hey, do you want to go to this concert with me tonight?" he asked.

Ophelia nodded again. *Sure, why not?* she thought. He might have some cute friends. They went to the concert that night, stealing glances back and forth while the band played loudly. Ophelia tried to focus on the music, but she couldn't help noticing Brandon staring at her from time to time. He hadn't invited her there as a friend.

The night ended with him playing the guitar in his living room while Ophelia sat and watched. Before she could make herself leave, he walked toward her with the powerful stride and kissed her. He swooped her up and carried her up his stairs to kiss her more. The attraction between them was undeniable. Ophelia had never felt the sort of chemistry and attraction she felt with Brandon. They didn't need words when their bodies connected; they knew instinctively what to do. Ophelia's thoughts, morals, and the strength she'd built toward protecting her heart went out the window. With him, time stood still; it was only the two of them in that moment. She knew she had to get away. But somehow she always ended up with him again. There were many romantic nights filled with powerful moments between them. But when the passion faded, Brandon was unsure of where to go next, and Ophelia grew scared and ran away.

He took her under what felt like a spell. She fell in love him so quickly. She had admiration for the man she saw in him, and she loved the man she knew he had the potential to be. He saw her and understood her too. He knew the pieces of her and solved the puzzle so quickly. Those before him saw her but never understood her. She was always told she was complicated or hard to understand. He figured her out quickly though. She put trust in him immediately, ignoring all signs of caution flashing in front of her. He had the capability to make her the happiest she could be, and she knew that and that's what would crush her to pieces.

Brandon made promises. He would break it off with the other girl—he just needed time to make things right for him and Ophelia. Though she wanted to believe him, she had her doubts. She hated to admit it, but her gut feelings were always dead on, and she didn't feel great about many of the things Brandon said. In the end, Ophelia had to cut off their romance. Fall was fading by then, and she watched the winter season blowing in as she put distance between herself and Brandon.

"This storm is pretty bad. You need to wait it out at least twenty minutes before you head back to Dallas. You going to be okay here by yourself?" asked Mickey. It was late in January and not the typical time of year you see storms like this in Texas.

"Yes. I think so. Don't worry. You all head on back. I'll be fine." Ophelia said, trying to give Mickey a confident smile.

The tornado sirens had stopped about ten minutes earlier. Mickey gave O a quick kiss on the cheek and grabbed his wife's hand as they ran out of the tiny Arlington private airport, through the rain, and into the car to head to Fort Worth.

Ophelia sat on a chair in the crowded airport and looked at her weather app on her iPhone. The storm had just passed them, but it was moving in the direction of her pathway home that night back to Dallas. It was late. The Cowboys had lost the playoff game that would have taken them to the NFC championship. She looked around only to see lots of people trying to figure out when they would get their airplane off the ground. She knew no one and felt scared and alone all at the same time. She fumbled a text message to Brandon, knowing he'd been at the game.

In the moments she felt afraid or alone, it was Brandon's face flashing through her mind. It brought her such a sense of comfort just to know he was somewhere nearby. She hadn't spoken to him since she'd run off that night, but she imagined he'd come and save her and tell her it was going to be okay. He'd hold her the way he had so many of those nights they were together. But immediately after the message sent, doubt sank like a stone in her stomach. He wouldn't come for her tonight, or any other night, for that matter. He'd made his choice about her from the moment he met her.

"You look like you could use a friend," an elderly man said as he sat down next to an almost weeping Ophelia. "Don't worry, darling. The storm will pass. It always does. And then we pick up and move on with it."

Ophelia gave the man a weak smile and thanked him for his kind words. Would this storm pass her? She just wanted it to be over with. Her phone buzzed, and she looked down. It was a text from Mickey's wife: *You better head back now. There's an even bigger storm coming right behind, but you've got a window to get home.*

Ophelia ran to her car in the pouring rain, jumped in, and fired the ignition. She pulled out of the Arlington private airport where Mickey had landed his plane earlier and started her drive back to Dallas. As she drove the interstate back to Dallas, both hands shaking on the wheel and tears streaming down her face, her thoughts drifted. There she was—thirty, beautiful, accomplished. She had set out to achieve her dreams. She was the strong woman she aspired to be. She had done it all on her own. And yet, she didn't have the love she'd always longed for.

She thought about Brandon and the rest of them, all the men who had come before him. O would never understand how they could claim she was the most amazing woman yet could never be there for her. What was she doing wrong? Had she not told them that she cared or loved them enough? No, it wasn't that. Something in the stars just hadn't aligned. Timing was always right for her, yet never right for them. She'd never understand why she'd continue to be put through so much disappointment in love. She continued to learn the hardest lessons. She always questioned if she was good enough. She had worked so hard to get where she was; she couldn't let this bring her down.

Though Brandon didn't come for her that night, he did come back. He promised her it was over with the other girl, that he wanted to start new . . . but he still needed time to figure things out. They spent the evening together after a long time apart. It felt good, like a new beginning. But it didn't take long for Ophelia's doubts to creep back in. She wanted to believe Brandon, but she knew he was still hiding something.

Eventually, Ophelia said goodbye to him for a second time and drove out to Barb's the following morning. She hadn't seen her in what seemed like ages. As she made the drive out to her mother's horse farm, she felt as though she was shattering inside. The last six months had crushed her, and she knew Brandon was to blame. Ophelia never felt he meant to break her heart, but he had. She thought of her words to him the night before. She'd finally written him off for good.

"I can't do this anymore."

That phrase felt all too familiar. Every time she opened her heart to a man, she watched him treat it poorly. Ophelia always ran when she smelled danger. She knew it was time to pick up and move on. This man had put her under a spell and weakened her in so many ways.

Ophelia pulled into Barb's long driveway. She went in to see Barb in the kitchen. Bill was out in the stables cleaning up. Barb had made an elegant lunch, but before she could put it on the table, she saw on Ophelia's face that something was wrong. Her daughter looked tired and worn out.

She'd spent most of the night crying her eyes out.

"Let's take a walk," Barb said, grabbing a bottle of chardonnay and two glasses.

"None for me today, but thanks," Ophelia said as she motioned her hand away.

Barb and Ophelia took a long walk through Barb's land while Barb's horses ran in the fields around them. Neither of the women said much. But in a rare glimpse, Ophelia saw Barb in her happy place. There she was standing on her land, wine glass in hand, with a smile on her face as she watched her horses run through the fields. She had a man who loved her in her stables, helping her keep up the home they'd built together. O smiled, happy to finally see her mother at peace. Their relationship had healed, and they could be friends now.

They got back to the main house, where Barb served them both the tiered cobb salad she'd put together and the homemade tuna dip.

"Okay, so what's the deal? You look beaten down," Barb said.

"I don't know. I'm thirty, and I guess this just isn't where I thought I'd be. The younger Ophelia would be so disappointed in me today," Ophelia said quietly, looking down at her salad.

"You need to find that great love in your life, Ophelia. You've always focused on other things, and meanwhile you let these losers crawl in and out of your life. Those men never appreciated you," Barb said.

"I guess. It's more than that, though. Work doesn't

motivate me anymore. It's a beat down every time I walk into the office. I don't feel like I'm accomplishing anything anymore. Maybe I should leave and start over somewhere else." Ophelia felt her life was falling apart everywhere she turned.

"All right, stop. I'd like to have my daughter back now please. You have worked too damn hard and sacrificed way too much of your time devoted to this career of yours. You're not giving up now. You're so close to getting everything you wanted out of your career. Why give up now? And let me remind you that I didn't raise you to give up. I raised you to be a strong woman. Take a long vacation. Do whatever you need to do to get your head back on straight. But once your head is back on straight, stay motivated to accomplish what you set out to do."

Barb and Ophelia didn't agree on much, but Barb did have a way of reminding Ophelia of who she was. And Barb was right. She did need to get away—away from her day-to-day life and away from Brandon.

Ophelia made plans to go to the only place she knew could heal her.

She landed at the Salt Lake City airport for the long President's Day weekend. Back on the ground, she turned her phone on. There it was, a voicemail from Brandon. It'd been weeks, and she had already begun to put him behind her. She played the voicemail as she walked off the plane and immediately ran into the bathroom. She felt she was going to throw up. She splashed cool water on her face only to look up in the mirror to see her chest had completely broken out in hives. Ophelia couldn't deny it anymore, the destructive force Brandon was in her life.

There in the Salt Lake City airport, the physical reaction of her relationship with Brandon was staring her in the face.

"Should I call him?" Ophelia asked Kate when she reached Kate's house that night. Ophelia played the voicemail for Kate a couple of times. "I mean, he sounds sincere."

Kate poured them both a glass of wine, and they sat on the couch cuddled up underneath the blankets, watching the snow fall outside the window.

Kate saw something changed in Ophelia. "This one has really gotten to you. I've never seen you like this before. I'll tell you one thing—from the sound of that voicemail, that man treasures you."

Ophelia had a lot to think about. She spent the next three days skiing with Peter, who had come in to stay with Kate and Calvin that weekend, as well. She needed to get her mind off of things back home, but her thoughts kept returning to Brandon. Was the story between them really over?

"So tell me about the guy. Kate says there's some guy you're all hung up on," Peter said as they got onto the chairlift at the mountain.

"Well, I've walked away twice already because he doesn't know what he wants or how he feels about me," Ophelia explained. "Now he is asking to be in my life again."

Ophelia told Peter the story of Brandon. He sat quietly, nodding and listening closely. He waited until she finished before he provided his reaction to her story.

· · ·

"Can I give you some advice, kid? Once is a mistake, twice is a coincidence, but the third time? Honey, that's a fucking pattern. I know the women in your family well. If you all have one thing in common, it's this—you are strong and beautiful women who deserve a man who will treat you all like the princesses you are. Any man would be lucky to be with you. If he can't see that—if he can't give you what you want, what you deserve—then do me a favor and leave his ass behind."

They reached the top of the chairlift and raced each other down the mountain. Completely out of breath, they rode the next chairlift up. Ophelia picked up the conversation where they'd left off.

"So, if we're so wonderful, why not Kate back then?" O asked Peter. Though the story between Peter and Kate had ended long ago, she'd always wondered what happened between them in the past.

"Kate is one of the great loves of my life. She's one of my best friends. I was too selfish back then to be the man she needed, though. Luckily we both ended up with the right people, and I think we are where we're supposed to be. Life has a funny way of working out. But know this, O —even after everything we've been through, I'd do anything for that woman."

After her conversation with Peter, Ophelia knew she just had to trust that things would end up as they should be. All she could do was follow her heart. The day before she left to return home, Kate and Ophelia spent hours sitting at a small bar in Park City, evaluating the whole situation. The question came down to this: Should Ophelia put her heart on the line that one last time?

Ophelia returned home to Brandon after that weekend, willing to try everything all over again and see where the path could lead. It was a rocky road, but she was willing to go in for one more try. Though her mind told her to walk away, her heart and gut wanted her to stay with him.

A few weeks later, Ophelia and Brandon landed in Las Vegas together. Brandon's wild lion eyes lit up at the sight of Sin City. Ophelia hated Las Vegas but did not have the heart to tell Brandon. It was his idea to go there. O clung to the fact that this would be the last-chance effort to steer the special force between them on a real path.

"Just go and have fun," Amy said to Ophelia earlier that day while she was packing up her things. "He's messed up a lot. And we've decided to give him one last try. But make sure you have a good weekend. If anything makes you upset, don't show it. Text it to me. We'll deal with it when you get back."

They had an incredible weekend together. They knew how to entertain one another, and they created memories only they would share. At dinner the last night, Brandon reached across the table and took both of Ophelia's hands in his. Ophelia held her breath. This was it. He would finally tell her he had chosen her.

"O, you're one of my most favorite people on this planet. You are so kind, so beautiful, never judgmental, intelligent, and so damn ambitious. I admire the woman you are and the woman you are aspiring to be every day. You make me want to be a better man." He dropped her hands and went back to eating.

Ophelia stared back blankly, unable to decipher what

he had just told her. He couldn't tell her the one thing she wanted to hear.

A few minutes later, Brandon got up and left the dinner table for a few minutes. Ophelia sat there by herself, staring off into space. She couldn't piece it together. Everything between them felt right, but he seemed off.

"Where did he go?" the man sitting at the table next to them asked Ophelia, breaking into her thoughts.

"Oh, I think he went to the restroom." Ophelia stared off. He had been gone for quite some time now.

As she said this, Brandon reappeared, making his way back to their table.

"I'm going to talk to him," the man said, getting up from his table. "A man never leaves a woman like you by herself . . . especially in Las Vegas."

Ophelia never knew what that stranger said to Brandon, but he came back to the table apologizing for his long absence. It didn't make a difference, though. That night was the final nail in the coffin for her. She knew then he'd never choose her.

After dinner, they went dancing, and Brandon slipped away, only to return with drugs he'd purchased for himself. It never bothered Ophelia that he did drugs recreationally. It was never her thing, but she accepted that Brandon liked to have a good time. She, however, did not expect that he'd try to put cocaine up her nose. She swatted his hand away, but the powder landed in her mouth. Everything came rushing up, and she felt physically ill.

Ophelia loved this man, but he was not right for her. He was never going to take care of her like she deserved.

He escorted her back to their hotel room, where he put her to bed and then left for the night to go play poker downstairs till the early hours of the morning while Ophelia slept the night away.

They were on their way home, sitting at the Las Vegas airport, when the end played out.

"So I guess this over between us, huh?" Brandon said.

"That's your choice," O replied.

"No, that's your choice," Brandon countered, clearly annoyed.

"Technically, it's yours."

Brandon rolled his eyes.

Ophelia looked at him long and hard. "What do you want, Brandon? Because now is the time to say it."

It was the moment of truth for her.

He sighed heavily. "I need to figure myself out," he admitted, staring away from her. He couldn't even look her in the eye.

Ophelia's heart sank, and she spoke softly, "And I can't wait around for you anymore."

The plane ride home was the longest three hours of silence. Ophelia sat there next to him with her head on his shoulder. Brandon's hand was wrapped strongly around her leg. He didn't let go of her the entire flight home. She knew this would be the last time she would be close to him like this. She felt her heart breaking all the way home. Her lion, the man she'd fallen for, did not love her in return. By the time they walked out of the airport toward home, tears were streaming down her face.

Things moved quickly after that. Brandon told O several nights later that he never felt the same for her.

He'd make her feel as if every feeling she ever had for him was a joke. He'd already broken her heart, but hearing that she meant nothing to him and wasn't worth fighting for broke her even more.

"I'm not sure where all this is coming from, O. I mean, Ophelia, sugar, we were always just supposed to be friends. We were having fun. That's all." Brandon said these things in his calm, cool attitude, like there had never been anything worthwhile between them.

Ophelia told him he was selfish and lost and that he brought out the worst in her. In many ways, she meant it, but probably not the way he interpreted it. He grew angry and tired of talking to her. They made the decision to part ways and never see or speak to one another again.

After they ended the call, O stared at the ceiling all night, unable to move. The next day she felt a heartbreak she'd never felt before. It was the first time in a long time that she could barely get out of bed. She managed to get out of bed and go for a run that morning only to break down in tears halfway through. She limped back to her house and took a shower, crying the whole time. She spent almost the entire day in bed crying on and off. That day, Ophelia decided she'd be as sad as she wanted, but tomorrow she'd get up and move on with her life.

"If he watched you walk away with tears in your eyes, then he doesn't care for you, O. You need to walk away from this one for good. I've never seen you torn up over a guy like this before. This is going to be really tough for you, but you have to stick to your guns and keep your head held high. This is just a bad chapter in your life. It will pass, I promise," Kate said over the phone as she listened to Ophelia cry that night.

And Ophelia did realize that she deeply loved him. Not in a childish, girlish way. She wanted nothing but his happiness and to see him move forward. If that meant they weren't in each other's lives, she was okay, so long as he was out there somewhere, happy. He'd never be there for her, and he'd never care for her the way she cared for him, so she made the decision to love her lion from afar.

"You've always seen the good in people, and that's what we all love about you, but it's also why so many men take advantage of you," Amy said on the phone to O a few nights later. "I just don't understand how you can still be in love with someone who hurt you that badly."

"I see him for who he is, Ames. I see the good, the bad, and the ugly. I know the man he is, and I know the man he has the potential to be. He does have a heart. He just doesn't value what is in front of him, unfortunately. I'll always care for him. But he's not good to me. I've worked too hard on my happiness to let someone bring me down the way he does. I made the choice, Ames. I'm moving on from him. It's just the best thing for me right now. But that doesn't mean I won't stop caring about what happens to him."

Ophelia locked Brandon away on a shelf with the other love stories in her life. He'd brought out the fun-loving spirit in her. He had shown her that she could love another person in the most selfless of ways. She had put his happiness above her own. And he'd shown her that she deserved so much more. She wouldn't stop trying to find it.

She had to get angry and let it all out. She missed the good times, the conversations, and the laughs they shared. But she didn't miss the tears, confusion, and betrayal. She didn't miss being taken advantage of and feeling physically unwell.

She always thought if she loved Brandon enough, he'd be better and that he would choose her in the end. But this story was over. It was time for her to drift away. She wished Brandon love and light. She hoped one day he'd live a more honest and truthful life and set out to be the man she knew he could be.

She just wouldn't be part of it. He was not her love story. He was her lesson.

Ophelia stumbled across a quote one day that made her smile: "If you can love the wrong person that much, imagine how much you can love the right one."

There was still hope that man was out there waiting for her.

15

SLIPPING AWAY

It was the summer of "Holy shit, I'm in my thirties now" for Ophelia. She had turned thirty the year prior, but the reality of it all hadn't really sunken in until she was nearing her thirty-first birthday. She was coming down off yet another failed romance, holding another piece of her broken heart that was trying to heal.

On a long plane ride up to Oregon, she sat and made a deal with herself to put it all behind her for good. She sat in silence most of the way, staring at the seat in front of her. How had she gotten here? Though she had accomplished things in her life, she hadn't nearly accomplished enough, and she damn sure wasn't where she thought she'd be at this point in her life. Her heart didn't even seem whole anymore. It'd been broken and let down so many times she didn't think it'd ever fully beat again—not the way it once had. She just wanted someone to love her, someone she could love in return. She'd dreamt of him her whole life and always thought he'd come for her. She been fooled so many times, thinking he'd already arrived.

"He hasn't come yet. You haven't met this man yet. I know this," Amy said to her one night after O had just about dried up all her tears from the last breakup. Ophelia's last bit of hope was slowly starting to slip away, so she remained focused on the only thing she had learned how to do—always better herself and make herself as happy as she could.

She stared out the window to the mountains. It was the long July Fourth weekend, and she'd be landing in Oregon soon. She was meeting Barb and Lillian, the first time she'd be reunited with both of them in a long time. Barb's recent adventure was purchasing a home tucked away in the mountains of Oregon. Though she hadn't fully left her life in Texas behind, she'd toyed with starting a new life out here. Barb had somehow convinced Lillian to get on an airplane and fly across the country to come see it. Lillian rarely left the house these days, so it was miracle she had agreed to the proposal.

Ophelia knew this might be one of the last times they'd get to spend time together, so she and Trenton had both made it a point to go out there. Trenton was out on his latest Alaskan adventure and planned to meet the women at Barb's house on his way back to Texas. Ophelia was barely able to take the time off and was lucky just to get to fly in for a few days.

Ophelia landed at the airport that afternoon with several text messages from Barb informing her she was outside holding up traffic at the airport waiting to pick her up. Ophelia had made the decision to leave all her mental baggage behind and just embrace the next few days ahead.

She walked out of the airport to find Barb and Lillian waiting for her. It'd been a couple of years since she'd seen Lillian. Age had made her grandmother even more fragile. Lillian looked as though she had just given up. She looked irritated to be there, away from her home. But she seemed happy to be with her grandchildren at least.

Barb was as happy as she could be. Life had turned out all right for her after all. O had noticed that she'd significantly cut back on her drinking over the past couple of years. Her life with Bill had settled into a new normal, and now Barb was starting to do all the things she had ever wanted to do with a man by her side.

The relationship between Barb and Ophelia had improved over the years. Maybe it was Ophelia getting older. She just found herself accepting things more easily with each passing year. While Barb still drove her nuts, she had come to terms with what her relationship with Barb was. They'd never be close, but they at least had a friendship.

It was her relationship with Lillian where Ophelia had failed. Her grandmother had done so much for her in her early years, but as Lillian grew more set in her ways, Ophelia had struggled to find her own identity, and the bond they'd once shared had slipped away. Lillian spent her days living with Dee and Chuck and hardly ever left the house. It was a nice escape for Lillian to break away and spend some time with Barb, Trenton, and Ophelia, despite the long travel to the Pacific Northwest.

The first night there, Lillian, Barb, and Ophelia

watched the sun set over the mountains. Lillian and Ophelia sat mostly in silence while Barb went on and on talking about who knows what. Barb never quite knew how to shut her mouth. She was always full of stories. It didn't bother Ophelia anymore.

She'd just let Barb talk.

"Does your mother ever shut up?" Lillian leaned over and said to Ophelia.

Ophelia laughed and gave her a nudge.

The group drove to Crater Lake the next day when Trenton arrived. There they stood, three generations of Harolds marveling at the natural beauty. Nature always had a calming effect on Ophelia. She could stare at it for hours at a time and feel the wounds of her heart healing one by one.

Lillian had another national park to check off her list and covered herself in cameras and binoculars, as usual. Ophelia giggled, thinking her grandmother looked like the elderly paparazzi. She couldn't have imagined seeing another national park without Lillian, though. It'd been years since they'd spent time together, and neither would have wanted to make the trip alone.

That night, when Lillian and Ophelia were alone on the patio watching the sunset again, their conversation took a surprising turn. Maybe it was Lillian reaching the age she was. Maybe it was the beautiful Oregon mountains surrounding them. But that night Lillian opened up to Ophelia about the man who had been her life from her own perspective and not the stories that she'd heard. Lillian opened up about her marriage to Carl. Although she had loved him dearly, in a way she always felt he held her back from being the independent woman she craved to be. She was never allowed to have an opinion during her married years.

Ophelia was shocked, but she stayed quiet and let her grandmother continue.

She went on to explain her reasoning for raising Dee, Barb, and Kate the way that she had. She had every intention of raising three alpha females. She wanted to see her daughters set out to live their lives independently, without the need for a man to tell them what to do. So much of it made sense to Ophelia in that moment. It was all intentional. The women in her family were raised to be tough. They were raised to push the envelope. Lillian had raised them to think freely in their relationships and never let a man walk all over them.

In turn, Ophelia opened up to Lillian, sharing about her depression for the first time. Although it was something she had overcome, she still had to fight to keep it at bay. The disorder was suppressed in her, but it never fully went away. Lillian had learned to live with it like it was just a part of her and accepted the way she felt, day in and day out. She accepted where she was and had learned to cope with it.

The conversation then turned to Dee. It had been years since Ophelia had seen her too. Life had gotten in the way. As a result, she'd missed what had been happening to her aunt. Lillian explained how bad Dee's depression had gotten over the last couple of years. She was becoming increasingly more unhappy each day.

"She wakes up every morning and starts drinking now. And the smoking hasn't gotten any better. I hate to say this, but Dee is not going to be with us much longer. I'm going to outlive my own daughter," Lillian said, staring off into the distance. She said it so calmly, as if it just rolled off her tongue like any other normal conversation.

Ophelia couldn't begin to understand. Dee was always the one trying to uplift everyone around her. She was always the one trying to mend their broken relationships. She was the one always offering a shoulder to cry on. No one had ever thought to look out for Dee herself.

"Is she okay?" Ophelia asked as Barb joined them on the patio.

"She's depressed and too stubborn to change her ways or do anything about it," Lillian explained.

Ophelia knew all about stubbornness. All the women in her family shared that too. None of them ever could admit things so easily.

Lillian explained how Dee rarely left the house. She rarely changed out of her bathrobe half the time. She just spent her days sitting at the kitchen table, drinking her chardonnay and smoking her cigarettes and staring off into space.

"I didn't realize it was that bad with Dee," Ophelia said to Barb as she cleared the dishes later that evening. Barb and Dee were best friends. Ophelia was shocked that her mother hadn't brought this up to her before.

"Well, she's sad. There's nothing really we can do about it," Barb said. There wasn't much for Barb to say, but Ophelia saw the fear in her eyes.

Ophelia returned home a few days later, still mulling over her conversation with Lillian. She sent Dee a text to tell her she loved her. Dee had always taken the time to look after Ophelia from afar. She just always wanted everything to be all right, for everyone to get along.

Ironic that in the end it was Dee who needed saving. A short two months later, Ophelia got the call that Dee had gone into a coma and had been hospitalized. All the alcohol and smoking had taken its toll on Dee's body, and her organs were beginning to shut down for good.

Barb, Kate, and O rushed to her bedside as fast as they could. They found Chuck there, completely falling apart as Lillian stared blankly at the wall. There was no hope for Dee surviving. Chuck loved Dee more than anything in the world. Watching her in that hospital room would forever change him, seeing the love of his life slowly start to slip away. Barb and Kate sat by their sister's side in the intensive care unit.

That night Ophelia found Barb on her hands and knees sobbing on the bathroom floor. "I'm going to lose my best friend," Barb said through her tears. Kate joined them on the floor, and the women held each other and cried.

Part of them felt that Dee meant to do this. She was so unhappy that she felt no need to go on. Could they have saved her?

The biggest heart in the family, the one who always held it together, was giving up and slipping away from them. The women broke that night, huddled together on the bathroom floor, as they struggled to understand how they could have done things differently.

Through all the times Barb and Kate had fought over the years, it was the first time Ophelia saw the sisters connect. As the hours passed, Kate held Barb in her arms.

Dee would die a week later.

16

THE NEW NORM

I t was at Dee's memorial that Ophelia came to realize her family had fallen part. Maybe it had been like that for the last decade; she couldn't know. Kate was right—Dee really was the glue that had held them all together throughout the years. Through all the conflict, drama, tears, name-calling, and damage, somehow she always knew how to bring the pieces back together and remind them they were family.

Ophelia watched as Barb and Kate took turns giving their tributes to their older sister they both loved so dearly. It was probably the only thing they ever agreed upon in their entire lives. Lillian sat in her chair in the front row. She was starting to forget a lot these days. Ophelia knew she wouldn't be with them much longer. She outlived her daughter, just as she predicted a few short months ago. At this point she'd watched so many of her loved ones that Ophelia thought she probably didn't have any tears left.

The men stood and watched from different corners of

the room. Chuck was lost and with no willpower to move on. He had lost his soul mate and the love of his life. He barely made it to Dee's memorial that night. He could not come to terms with the fact that she was gone. It took much of Barb and Kate's pleading to get him there. Ophelia always found their relationship odd. Though had a rough way of speaking to one another, at the end of the day they shared an unconditional love.

Mickey and Trenton stood not far behind her, a supportive shield over Ophelia, as usual. Mickey came to the memorial to support the family and say goodbye to Dee. She had always been a friend to him. And he wanted to be there for Trenton and Ophelia. Though Ophelia never looked back, she knew Trenton and Mickey were just a few steps behind her.

Barb had lost it since Dee's passing. The emotional, fragile woman Ophelia had grown up with had returned tenfold. Barb took her emotion and anger out on everyone in the wake of Dee's death. Ophelia got the brunt of Barb's emotional outburst most of her life, so for her this was normal. Kate always came in a close second. But the outbursts were projected even further now. Barb took her anger out on Trenton and Bill too. Ophelia always thought Bill was a saint for hanging in with Barb the last ten years. But she worried about him now. How much more could he take? *A man can only be put down by his woman so many times before he leaves for good*, Ophelia thought. That was the thing about resentment, it grew and grew until it overcame your love for a person. Depression was a selfish sickness. Her mother never had been able to see very far beyond herself. She failed to see how her behavior affected others.

More than ever, Ophelia felt this was the time to begin a life of her own for good. "I don't want to end up like them," she confided to Mickey over dinner weeks later. "I don't want to be so sad that I watch my life slip away or I alienate people around me."

Mickey put down his fork and looked straight into Ophelia's eyes so she knew he meant it. "You won't. You have strength in you that none of them have."

Ophelia felt the truth of this. She was strong. It was there, but she didn't yet know how to use that strength. It was time for her to turn inward. Time for her to pull it all out and become the woman she wanted to be. She was so focused on not being sad that she hadn't really worked on building the life she wanted. She still hung onto her life as it was, trying to fix the past instead of focusing on the present, instead of walking confidently into her future. She was clinging to fixing her current life instead of building the life she wanted. She was determined to devote herself to building the life of her dreams. She loved the women in her life. They'd built her. She appreciated the pieces of Dee, Lillian, Kate, and Barb that she carried within her. She had learned from them. They had become some of her life's greatest teachers. But it was time to walk her own path.

As for men, it was time to let them all go for good. All the love stories of her past. She hung onto all of the moments, all the heartbreak, and all the memories for too long. She knew she had to let it all go. She'd kept them all up on a shelf. She'd wonder about these men from time to time: Where were they? Had they found true happiness? Was it all worth it? Ophelia had spent the greater part of the last several years letting everything else go. But she'd never let go of her love life. It was a dark road twisted within the shadowed regions of her heart. There were bright spots along the way where she'd held some of her happiest memories, but the journey was a rugged one, and she didn't want to walk that road again. She didn't want to revisit the memories anymore. She'd hung onto them for so long.

Ophelia longed to just "be." To stand still in the meadow even if it meant standing alone. She was tired of trying. They'd all found her, but they'd left her too. Life didn't always turn out the way you imagined it when you were young, and this was the hardest lesson of all. Ophelia had to learn to let go of the fairy tale and live the life she'd been given. A happy life, filled with friends and family and a career to be proud of. She had herself, and that would have to be enough. She'd have to stop chasing the fairy tale.

She had spent the last several years running from a home instead of making a home. She'd fallen back in love with the city that had raised her. Her career and her life were on the track she wanted, and she finally felt free to have the life she'd always dreamed of.

In time, Barb moved past her grief and focused on life with Bill. Kate carried on in her life with Calvin. Through all their time together, their love grew stronger year after year. Lillian found contentment in the long years she'd put into her life. Maybe the tragedy she carried was meant to guide Ophelia and the others, to set them on the right paths.

. . .

Ophelia sat happily in a cozy corner on a cold Texas night at her favorite French restaurant right down the street from her home. She was so happy to have fallen in love with this city again. She'd come to this restaurant a lot lately. It was her happy place away from home. She sat contentedly, smiling at all she had. She was where she should be, and everything that happened was part of her story.

And then it happened.

"Excuse me . . . I don't mean to interrupt, but you're Ophelia, correct?"

Ophelia looked up. She blushed at the sight of the tall, handsome, dark-haired man looking down at her.

"Yes, I am. And you are?"

"I'm David. I've been waiting to meet you for a long time," he said, grabbing an empty chair and sitting down across from her.

She recognized him. She had seen him from afar a time or two. But she always was distracted by something or someone.

At that moment, she knew. The arrow Mickey told her about had hit her, finally. The final piece of the puzzle had revealed itself. He had come for her.

"So have I."

THANK YOU

If you enjoyed reading *Strength of Her Heart*, please leave a review at the store you purchased it from.

Reviews are the best way to show your support for an author and to help new readers discover their books.

Made in the USA
Lexington, KY
16 February 2019